Newcastle
Short Story Award

I0594421

HUNTER
WRITERS
CENTRE

First published in Australia in 2021 by Hunter Writers Centre
www.hunterwriterscentre.org
Newcastle Short Story Award Anthology 2021
ISBN 978-0-6488504-4-1

Cover photograph:
Newcastle Harbour by Carol Swadling

Published by Hunter Writers Centre Inc. 2021

Hunter Writers Centre
Newcastle NSW 2300

hunterwriterscentre.org

HUNTER
WRITERS
CENTRE

Contents

Judges' report

Amanda O'Callaghan and Jay Carmichael

Hundreds of Australian writers from across the country and beyond trusted us with their work. It was an honour to read and assess this large pool of short stories for the 2021 Newcastle Short Story Award. Congratulations to the prize-winners, and well done to all the longlisted writers whose work is published in this anthology.

As we live in different states, the judging process was done via multiple emails and, as our lists got shorter, by a series of online meetings. The stories that made their way into this anthology have been read multiple times, by both judges, as we sifted through the work in search of our winners. Our tastes differed. This was a good thing. We both returned to stories we might otherwise have passed over. While we acknowledge that the judging of any competition has a subjective element, we were united in our quest for strong, clear voices, even in the quietest of stories. Our respective longlists had many overlapping entries. Where choices did not coincide, we each 'fought' for stories that we thought had merit. Judging a substantial award well is hard work, and we can assure every entrant that their story was considered with interest and respect. Inevitably, many submissions must be rejected. It was disappointing to have to automatically disqualify a number of good stories that exceeded the word limit or were submitted with author names attached. All the stories for the award were judged blind. Themes often emerge, and this year we found that children, miscarriage, domestic violence, and bushfires featured strongly. Some of our winning stories have explored these topics.

We are delighted with the eclectic scope of the stories published in this year's anthology.

The winning stories are noticeably different in style and theme, but display flair, confidence and a genuine proficiency in the tricky business of short story writing. For those who did not make that final list, it may help to know that there were many other excellent submissions that came extremely close. The diversity exhibited in this year's anthology pleases us enormously. It's a glimpse into the established and emerging talents of Australia's wonderful short story scene.

A note from Amanda

We are both delighted with this year's winner of First Prize. 'Swooping Season' is the story that never went away. When I first read it, I wrote in my notes: 'Excellent. Possible winner.' I found this story poignant and elegant. It was created by a writer entirely in charge of their craft. I loved the first line, the last line, the way the author held competing narratives in such a delicate and ultimately powerful way. I thought, at that first reading, that it would need a very good story to push it out of pole position. Many came close, but as the lists shortened there was no question that 'Swooping Season' would remain. Sincere congratulations to the author on this beautifully rendered story, which we both enjoyed very much.

In a strong field there is very little space between the awarded stories, and this proved to be true for the 2021 contest. Second Prize went to 'She Wore Red on her Lips', a marvellously vivid, aural story of loss and survival. 'Baby Oil', with its quiet dignity and pain, was awarded Third Prize. 'Chopping Wood' (Highly Commended) unfolds a tale of generational conflict and yearning, told with grace and skill. 'Scissor Tango', also Highly Commended, is one of a number of stories wreathed in bushfire smoke. It impressed us with its visceral, unexpected turns and its strong imagery. If 'Scissor Tango' evokes the whiff of bushfire smoke, 'White Water Glimpses' (Commended) explores the aftermath of a full conflagration, centring on a woman changed absolutely by the devastating impact of the fires: 'In the morning sun, the contours and ridgelines, once a soft wink behind canopy and understory, lay sharp, exposed, awful and unwanted in their clarity, like a parent seen naked for the first time in decades.' Also Commended was 'With Eyes to See', a surprising and poignant tale exploring the competing themes of tenderness and duty. 'Playing Hide and Seek' (Commended) is an important and affecting story of innocence and cruelty.

I hope you enjoy our choices. Thanks to the Hunter Writers Centre for this award, and to all who contributed this year. It was a pleasure to work alongside my co-judge, Jay Carmichael, as we explored the wonderful range of submissions. Keep writing!

A note from Jay

Restraint, imagery and voice were three things I found particularly pleasing in the entries to this year's Newcastle Short Story Award. It was a pleasure to judge this award with Amanda O'Callaghan—despite us being in different states, we managed to have robust and exciting conversations about writing and all it means to us.

Some of the words in this collection conjure images that I sensed so strongly it was as if I have lived through the scenes myself. It's remarkable, really, to think how a few random words arranged in a certain way can have such an effect. And yet, it can be so easy for writing to become too heavy in the images it's conveying. It takes a certain confidence within a writer to wield images and to know when to take the pen away from the page.

Such restraint can be seen in 'Baby Oil'—a taut re-telling of an encounter in a shared shower block. The sounds of crashing waves, the smell of honey and jojoba, the sight of skin and a baby being washed. There's a swirling sense in this story, as if you're trying to hold on to something that's not quite tangible enough: 'The baby gurgled as she laid him down and stripped off his duds and nappy, his feet waving in the air like dandelions in a breeze.' The author gives just enough detail, and just enough evocation, that I could not help but stay in that shared shower block, too.

'She Wore Red on Her Lips' could not be more different but it, too, has a rhythm. In this case, its sentences carry the repetition of 'she wore'—and surprising, delightful variations of this phrase: 'her housemates gathered in the parlour and wore her out with their gossip', 'While they speculated, she wore, she hoped, the face of a nun', 'Eventually she approved him, then another four: tick, tick, tick'. The rhythm is not contained to the structure of each sentence: it balloons out, giving shape to the whole history of a person in just short of 2,000 words. It's rather tumultuous writing—and, indeed, should be for this is a story about an entire life: its joy, its heartache, little wins, continuous disappointments and the quiet moments we hold within us.

'Playing Hide and Seek', a commended story, devastates us with the implicit meaning within the text. Its imagery evokes a sweeping landscape, on which lives have been born and destroyed. A key feature of this story is that, to some extent, it remains unresolved. What is left unsaid is just as strong as the writer's voice itself.

Voice, such as those in this collection, is a result of writing style. Writing style is, loosely, the conscious and subconscious application of writing techniques. What I hope this year's anthology does most of all is to showcase how vast and exciting writerly voices can be. Whether or not the technique is always spot on, whether there are small slips or missed opportunities. Let the voices in this collection carry you.

1st Prize donated by the University of Newcastle

2nd Prize donated by Hunter Writers Centre

3rd Prize donated by Westfield Kotara

Highly Commended donated by Catchfire Press

Highly Commended donated by Officeworks Kotara

Commended donated by Foghorn Brewhouse

Commended prize donated by Interflora

Commended prize donated by Booktopia

Swooping Season

Lucy Nelson

Winner, Newcastle Short Story Award

When Lorna was fourteen, the driver of a white station wagon drifted off to sleep and sailed in a dream along a dimly lit road, through the front of her parents' red hatchback and into their seated bodies.

In the weeks that followed, Lorna and Aunty Roe—her next of kin and sudden guardian—did little more than follow each other closely from couch to kitchen, shrinking their lives down to a few square feet, giving the dead space to die. They made neat piles of dirty plates. One helped the other find a pair of glasses or a matching sock. They sat still, staring at the room, until one needed to stretch. A slow dance of only the necessary. Lorna's first period arrived, entirely overshadowed. She scuffed to her mother's dresser drawer, dug her hand under a tangled nest of bras and plucked out a pad as though she'd been doing it all her life.

The sound could be all-the-way down but Lorna needed the TV on overnight. Otherwise, the house would fall to darkness as well as silence. Lorna and Roe lay beside each other on the couch, a square puddle of blue TV light across their chins and throats, voicing unconnected thoughts.

There are still some sandwiches, said Lorna.

She told me she had a dress on lay-by, said Roe. She was having second thoughts about the colour though.

Remember the shower takes a sec to get hot in the morning, said Lorna.

I've been trying to have a baby, said Roe.

Slowly they prepared to move to Roe's house by the sea. They considered staying in the city instead but the thought of sleeping beside her parents' empty bedroom each night was more unsettling to Lorna than any relocation. And the image of Aunty Roe in the city—with her thongs and her floppy sun hat—had an uneasy squeak about it, like a tennis shoe on concrete.

The couch at Roe's place, instead of the butter yellow linen her mother had chosen from a swatch book, was a faded cotton, salt-lake pink. Instead of going to bed straight after her homework, she and Aunty Roe watched dramas about handsome doctors or sassy detectives on the couch until they were sleepy enough to call a night a night. On Saturdays, instead of going to Teresa's house to play Consequences while rain drove the ants in, she dawdled to the waterfront under a blazing sun. The water was more grey than blue. Half-heartedly, almost by default, she had befriended three girls who were tall and quiet like she was. Together they sat on grass tufts near the beach and dug Minties from their teeth. Lorna tore the papers into long, crinkly strings while the others read the quizzes in *Dolly*: Are you ready to go all the way? Ice Queen or Drama Queen—What signals are you sending? Lorna laughed when they laughed, sighed when they sighed, feeling nothing in particular.

Concentration was impossible. Questions in textbooks were inky stains. The nearness of the ocean gave things a holiday feeling; surely nothing was expected of her here. She walked to and from school in a sticky stupor, feeling her nose grow pink, a coin-sized pool of sweat in the small of her back.

The other thing about the seaside was the nesting brown mother larks who swooped in the spring. It happened on her way home one afternoon and at first it was only an unexpected clip to the head. She thought someone had lobbed a tennis ball her way. She heard a small sound of surprise in her throat and froze on the spot, looking around for evidence but there was only the bird, coming back for a second go and she saw the perfect white segments of its underwing, single daisy petals pressed into neatly overlapping rows. She'd never thought of birds as having legs before. When she drew a bird, it was always an oval for a body with some three-pronged claws sticking out. But up close, overhead, a small brown muscular leg was flexing in the air. Missing her the second time, it landed on the grass in front and flew up from the ground instead, this time getting close enough to scratch a claw lightly up along her cheek. It settled high in a tree and watched for her next move. Hot tears stung her eyes. She tried to swallow but coughed wetly instead. She held her backpack up as a shield, put her head down and jogged the rest of the way home. Embarrassment flooded her warmly.

She was glad to find Roe's house empty. She stood at the bathroom mirror, flushed, examining the raised-up white graze on her cheekbone and cupping a sun-warmed hand over it. Her blood roared. She could feel it throb even in her fingernails as she sat shaking on the toilet seat and was greeted by the bright red sight of her second period. There were six months between bleeds.

The irregularity had gone unnoticed. The pain was worse this time. Lorna imagined her uterus as an old woman's face the moment after sucking on a lemon wedge and twisting to a contorted wrinkle, dribbling juice, spitting seeds.

She called one of the tall quiet girls on Roe's rotary phone to explain about the bird. Don't they swoop in the city? was all the girl said, and then she read out questions from a *Dolly* Quiz to take Lorna's mind off things. It was a quiz they'd already done at the beach that weekend but, this time, Lorna got a different result and she laughed hard when it told her she was a Tantalising Temptress instead of a Wary Wallflower. She laughed so hard she coughed up a splodge of white phlegm into her hand, closing her fingers over it until she hung up.

She caught the bus to school instead of walking after that. Through the window she saw people choosing to walk anyway and envied their bravery, some waving sticks over their heads to prevent the attacks. A family with three small children all wore hats made from white ice-cream buckets and carried a golf umbrella for extra protection. Cyclists threaded cable ties through the holes of their helmets. She grew accustomed to the spring parade of protective headwear from the safety of the vinyl bus seat. Anything can start to seem normal after time.

If it weren't for her parents' accident, she might have stayed in the city her whole life and never known the dreadful thrill of a territorial mother lark catching your hair in its hooked claw, or whomping the side of your face with the heft of its feathery body. Sometimes the birds got the timing wrong and the impact was only a densely packed whoosh of air right above your ear.

On Roe's couch, Lorna's afternoons flattened into evenings. In between TV shows there were previews of what to expect on the news. She put a tape in one night to record a report about swooping season. There was footage of a dust-coloured mother lark descending, a talon outstretched like a foot on a brake pedal. Later she watched the video in slow motion, pausing to look at the bird's eyes: small, hard, sharp with intention. On the news they said you shouldn't run when they swoop because it's the movement that startles them. If possible, you should look directly at them, make eye contact. The best thing, everyone seemed to know, was to feed them. They could recognise human faces and if they got to know you, they'd hop up close and eat raw minced meat right out of your hand. Aunty Roe did it sometimes in the garden and encouraged Lorna to try, but the thought of hand-feeding beef to a bird seemed gory, nightmarish. Somehow it only brought blood to mind.

Roe was trying to have a baby again. Lorna went with her sometimes to the appointments and looked at the other people in the waiting room.

We can have babies on our own now, Roe would always say. As long as you're healthy, it's okay. But Lorna had seen a graph at the fertility clinic: a line charting the likelihood of a healthy pregnancy floated buoyantly along the top of the graph until age thirty-five and then plummeted, almost dipping out of the picture entirely by forty, which Roe was by then.

The pregnancy ended unceremoniously. There was no fall, no clattering along hospital corridors on a jangly gurney, just Roe clutching her belly and bending over too much in the kitchen one Tuesday. There was blood, but not an alarming amount. Lorna would have expected more. Remember the baby was only the size of a robin's egg, said the nurse.

In the taxi home Lorna sat in the middle seat so she could put her chin near Roe's shoulder and share the same view through the passenger window. The driver touched the wheel so lightly that the car appeared to drift along of its own accord. The drive felt so long. Time had curled into a rolling ball of heavy eyes and dry lips without any changes in the light. But night must have been and gone because now it was hot and bright.

Lorna helped Roe out of the car, even though she was okay to walk. Roe went straight to the couch, slouched and numb from painkillers. *The Addams Family* was on TV. At the end, just before the credits, the camera zoomed in on a broken synthetic spider web, bloating in the fake studio breeze, before fading to black. How must it be to make your whole home from bodily stuff only to have that wrenched away too?

Lorna fell asleep on the couch that night. She dreamt that she was watching her mother in a black and white movie. She was doing ordinary round-the-house type things but had shrunk in size and could barely see over the bench tops. She had to climb a step ladder to reach the kitchen taps. Wanting to be with her, Lorna stood up from the sofa, checking her own body but finding that she was still her usual size, she guessed at how she might move through the screen and into the movie. She considered the holes in the speaker or the VCR flap, where Curly Sue got jammed once. But then she somehow knew for certain—as can happen in dreams—that the way to get there was to press her body close up against the screen and let the static crackle against her skin, zapping her, shrinking her and delivering her into the TV world with a fuzzy jolt. The crackling got so loud and the static was making all her hair stand on end but before the zap could deafen her, she clenched awake and sat up.

Aunty Roe was standing beside the whistling kettle, still and sleepy in her silk nightie, her breasts too small to fill the lacy triangular cups. Lorna sat up to check Roe's posture for signs of pain but there was only a deep yawn as she sensed Lorna waking and turned to look. Lorna yawned too. There's something wrong with my period, she said.

She got up and put the tape of the news story about swooping season into the VCR. She watched it again and again, pausing on the lark's face as it filled the screen. The dust-coloured mother, the eyes hardened and glazed, blind with fear.

She Wore Red On Her Lips

Kit Scriven

Second Prize

She wore red on her lips. She wore her jaw tilted. She wore her cheekbones high with her head turned slightly so her eyelashes might silhouette against the pale blue background of her horizon, the cover of *The Australian Women's Weekly*, the 5 July 1941 edition, which she kept rolled in a handbag she wore on a strap over her shoulder, ever handy for the tick, tick, tick. Tick.

She wore garters.

She wore a pout, red on her lips.

She wore her screams on the inside, mostly.

She wore nights when she almost convinced herself she belonged. She wore a line traced with eyebrow pencil on the backs of her thighs, knees and calves, all the way down to her ankles and the red promise of her dancing shoes. The war had worn down supplies—especially of nylon, and men—and a line drawn down the back of her legs was a line drawn. She wore her legs choreographed to a life that real stockings with real seams could never achieve.

She wore her Americans attached by a hook that contracted and expanded depending on how they looked at her, how she squirmed when they had the hook in her, alcohol, and the ingenuity of a line drawn on skin compared with its nylon substitute.

She wore convent walls. She wore solitude.

Her wardens wore a gaze profound and uncritical, and a confidence that could never have been gathered from the pages of *The Australian Women's Weekly*. They wore their eyes downcast; not for them the jut of eyelashes against an infinite horizon.

The nuns wore pity on the smooth of their faces. Around their faces and tucked back into their habits, the nuns wore white garlands seamed from a fabric that could not have been nylon. They wore their portable haloes with a placid humility that enraged their guest. They wore her anger. Inevitably, their martyrdom wore her down.

She wore their advice. She knitted bootees because babies wore bootees and the nuns told her that she'd feel better if she gave something. She wore her guilt in a bubble that floated between her and the world, in a strange membrane where she lived with her head perpetually cocked, listening for the receding wail.

She wore boots because the factory gave a discount. She wore callouses on her hands and a foreboding that this was it: somewhere to wait it out.

After work and on weekends she wore a rented room with a bed iron and narrow. She wore a floral dressing gown to a bathroom that stank of wet towels and seven boarders. She shared meals in a kitchen where her landlady—who never wore a halo, nor patience—served corned beef with watery mashed potatoes and cabbage, or sausages and onions with boiled potatoes and peas. The kitchen, the front hall, the passage, the lounge, her skinny bedroom, her hair, her clothes, even her boots—all wore the stink of cabbage and onion.

In the evenings, her housemates gathered in the parlour and wore her out with their gossip about the girl who had previously occupied her room and who had abruptly left the boarding house. While they speculated, she wore, she hoped, the face of a nun.

At night she lay between stiff sheets and listened to the clock in the hall and wondered if this was all it was: an accumulation of tick, tick, tick. Tick.

She wore her secret.

She wore a pout, red-painted on her lips. She wore her jaw tilted. She wore her cheekbones high with her head turned slightly sideways in the hope her eyelashes might silhouette against an horizon she could endure.

She wore the way the foreman looked at her. She wore his interest and the contempt of her workmates. Eventually, she wore him, because he had a hook made for the job and she thought he might fit.

She wore a housedress she'd seen in *The Australian Women's Weekly* and ticked off first the refrigerator, then the toaster, the radio, a set of cutlery in easy polish silver (with at least four of everything), and a dining suite featured in the 4 January 1947 edition: tick, tick, tick. Tick. Tick. She kept the magazine because the cover wore a portrait of a baby, who might have been a boy, and whose red-lipped, blue-eyed beauty would have set anyone's heart a-tick, a-tick, a-tick. A-tick.

Over nine years she wore five daughters and their suck, hydraulic at her breast.

She wore them on the inside, initially, then forever in an invisible membrane where she stored the cry of a baby carried by a nun along an endless corridor. She lived in a bubble of anxiety with whooping cough, fish bones, wet fingers in the vicinity of power sockets, teenage pregnancy, the cloy of the newsagent's fingers on her palm as he dispensed the change, the way he stared at her youngest daughter.

She wore gloves, leather and tailored to fit, because the nuns and *The Australian Women's Weekly* had taught her to believe.

That a hand could fit a glove.

That if she wore it long enough her life might fit.

She wore a handbag on a strap over her shoulder. Inside the handbag she kept her gloves and a purse in which she maintained a notebook with a page separate for each of the nuns, with one entry marked up in eyebrow pencil and bookmarked by a worn strand of wool—worn because she too often caressed the thread she had scissored from one of the bootees the nuns had encouraged her to knit.

She wore her hair long, brunette, then short cropped and blonde, then red for a while, to match her lips. She wore her hair in cuts that narrowed her face and flaunted her cheekbones.

She wore his fear.

She wore her hair in styles she invented, because the cuts in the magazines and the photographs in the hairdressers didn't have enough drape to confuse bruise with shadow.

She wore the shine off her wedding ring.

She wore red on her lips—the wet stuff she couldn't spare that had a taste of its own and made her wonder what it would be like to be strawberry, orange, lemon all the way through, and whether there was anything as brutal as having to taste your life, all the way through.

Her daughters wore store bought clothes because she couldn't knit after the nuns and the bootees.

Five baby girls wore her hands warm and cupped around the ball and instep of each foot. Each daughter woke decades afterwards in a terror of insight and knew that nothing would ever fit them like their mother's hands around the smooth of their feet.

When she'd turned enough pages of enough magazines a perpetual, self-reckoning irony wore its way into her soul: tick, tick, tick. Tick.

She wore her ticks on the inside until they spotted daylight at the corners of her eyes and mouth and ran for it. They didn't run far, just to the outside corners of her eyes and the droop at each end of her mouth, where she wore them while they dug in and waited for reinforcements.

She wore blue on her thighs in patterns she despised. She wore regret varicose on her legs and spent hours standing backwards to the mirror, transfixed by how her wild tributaries spiralled, intersected, and dead-ended. She wore rivers of grief and pulsing intersections and dead ends of conversations with a receding wail.

She wore the 1960s. She watched the black-and-white finality of the luck of the draw and wept for the conscripts who wore the misfortune of his birthdate. The newspapers listed the names of the boys who wore the glory of death, but never the names of their mothers.

She wore the seventies, Whitlam, and an end to the war, but not the unknowing. She wore Gough's gift of free tertiary education. The young men at the university wore the way she stared into their faces.

Before they married her daughters, her potential sons-in-law wore her examinations with affected patience, even her interest in their family history. One, who married her eldest daughter and who hinted that he might have been adopted wore special attention. Eventually she approved him, then another four: tick, tick, tick. Tick.

She wore the role of grandmother and the sometime love of grandchildren. She wore the bitterness of the foreman when she told him that you wore love until you discovered it didn't fit.

She wore her patience and its inevitable rupture.

She wore separation, divorce, and the incomprehension of her daughters and grandchildren and wondered for the rest of her life whether the explosion was worth it, because the receding wail was still there, along with the tick, tick, tick. Tick.

She wore the patience of the people at Births, Deaths and Marriages until they said we'll call you, because his record wore a mark that said he didn't want her to contact him, and she would have to wait for his tick, tick, tick. Tick.

She wore her exhaustion mute on her lips. She wore her jaw tucked in and her cheekbones angled down, and her face aimed straight at the pavement in case the jut of her eyelashes offended the horizon. She wore poverty without the vow, or humility, or any hope of martyrdom.

She lay between worn sheets and rehearsed a dream where he found her. He followed the line she'd marked for him in eyebrow pencil. He noted the scenes where she wore red on her lips, Americans, the foreman, his five sisters at suck at her breast, and the tick, tick, tick. Tick. He wore away much of her dream staring at the walls of the convent and the nuns.

He wore her ticks in the creases at the corners of his eyes and mouth. He wore a faded bootee in the top breast pocket of his suit, where other men wore bright handkerchiefs that matched their neckties.

She wore his palms on her cheeks and his thumbs under her jaw as he tilted her head to that angle that best flaunted her cheekbones. She wore his gaze as he stared into all that was his mother. He turned her head slightly, until she wore the jut of her eyelashes silhouetted against an horizon of infinite forgiveness.

Towards the end she wore spittle white on her lips. She wore the hands of a nun clasped around both of hers. She wore her hands as two fists, tight clenched, because that was the only way she could go.

The nun who maintained watch until the end wore a white halo tucked into her habit and a list that she wore pinned in a place behind her eyes. That night, the nun lay between stern sheets and added another tick against each item on her do-not-do list. She lay awake for a long time because *wondering* wasn't on the list. She wondered if this was all it was: an accumulation of tick, tick, tick. Tick.

Baby Oil

Alison Gibbs

Third Prize

We headed for the showers, my sister Vicki and me, picking our way through the tents and annexes with our shower bags and bath towels tucked under our arms. It was summer, 1973. It was six o'clock in the evening. There remained some warmth in the sun. People were still on the beach, but this was our time at the showers, time to get out of our cozzies and wash off the sand and salt while Mum got tea started back at the caravan.

Vicki was twelve. I was three years younger and still at primary school. She carried the amenities key on its big wooden paddle and I followed behind her, watching my feet, alert to the danger of guy ropes and tent pegs. The sand on the track was as fine as dust and stained a sooty grey by the tea trees. It was so fine and soft that our thongs barely left prints, except in the wet slurry around each tap along the way.

At the bottom of the hill, the path met the gravel road that lead up to the kiosk and amenities block. This stretch of road was where the surfies parked their vans, backing them into the dank shade behind the dunes. Kombis and panel vans covered in surfboard logos and pictures of busty women and hibiscuses. They were draped with towels and were sometimes pumping out music or thrumming with the sound of a single guitar.

We picked up speed along this stretch—we always did—Vicki increasing her lead and me pattering behind, barely stealing a glance as we hurried by. The girls who emerged from the back of these vans were nothing like the young women our mother expected us to become. Smooth, tanned, mussy-haired, wrapped in soft sarongs, they went about their business in the shadows of the dunes while, over on the beach, their boyfriends rode the waves. I found them fascinating and disturbing in equal measure. Even at my young age, I could read in their languid movements and long tangled tresses the suggestion of salty sex in the back of a kombi van.

The showers were busy already. We leaned against the raw brick wall and waited. The late afternoon sun slanted through the Besser blocks above our heads and the steamy air was sweet with the smell of moisturiser: honey and jojoba. We watched the women busy at the mirrors, leaning in with lip balm, combing out their hair, inspecting the sunburn on their shoulders. The showers roared behind the painted doors. From one came the piping voice of a child, her chubby feet now visible, stepping into the shortie pyjama pants that her mother held off the floor.

A key rattled in the lock and the door pushed open. A slim, blonde woman backed into the room pulling a bulky stroller in behind her. She wore a loose cotton shirt over a pair of denim shorts and her hair pulled up in a thick ponytail. Carefully, she manoeuvred the stroller around and wheeled it to the baby bath in the corner.

Vicki nudged me in the ribs. I slapped her hand away.

'It's Leigh Mathieson,' she whispered, trying not to move her mouth.

The woman was now fitting the plug into the deep steel tub. There was no mirror above it, just a sign—BABY BATH ONLY—but even from behind, it was suddenly clear that she was very young. Leigh Mathieson had been in the same year as our brother, Paul, who was now fifteen. I didn't know much about babies but the child looked to be about the right age. It was towards the end of first term, just before the May holidays, that the pregnancy had been discovered.

I didn't know her, still being in primary school, but Leigh Mathieson's pregnancy was big news at the time. She wasn't the first schoolgirl to get herself into trouble but she was nearly eight months gone when she went to the sick bay, feeling unwell, and Mrs King, the girls' mistress, had made her take off her jumper, revealing the straining box pleats of her beltless uniform. She'd covered it up all that time—not even her own mother knew, which was why our mother went on about it at the dinner table one night. How on earth could a mother not notice? What kind of a mother was she?

'Well—poor girl. Too late to do anything about it now. She'll have to go ahead and have it and adopt it out, I suppose.'

I found this comment puzzling. What could the poor girl have done if she hadn't left it so late? It was all very interesting to an eight-year-old like me, as Mum was only too well aware. When the conversation turned to who the father might be, she deftly intervened, steering us away from the biological facts. There was, however, a note in her voice that sounded like a warning: this is what happens when young girls don't respect themselves.

But that was the interesting thing: nobody thought Leigh Mathieson *was* that sort of girl. She was bright and athletic, the daughter of an accountant. We quizzed Paul about her but didn't get much from him. All he knew was that Leigh never came back to class. She just disappeared and we heard and thought no more about her until that January evening when she turned up with her baby in the showers at Budgeree Beach.

The doors of the five shower cubicles were painted different colours. The aqua one opened now and released the chatty child. The little girl went to the stroller and stared at the baby before following her mother out the door, scuffing through sandy sludge on the floor.

Vicki took the vacant cubicle. I was happy to wait, hugging my shower things to my chest and watching Leigh Mathieson. She leaned into the tub and tested the water with her elbow. From a bag hanging on the back of the stroller, she pulled out a padded mat and an enormous toiletry bag, from which she produced a bottle of *No More Tears* shampoo, baby powder, baby oil and a small box of tissues. Then came a towel and washer with blue bunnies on them and a small lemon hairbrush, like one you'd use on a doll. After setting these items out on the bench, she crouched in front of the stroller, unclipped the straps and heaved the child onto the changing mat. She peered at an angry mosquito bite on his doughy thigh and then drew him towards her and tugged his pale blue singlet over his head. The baby gurgled as she laid him down and stripped off his duds and nappy, his feet waving in the air like dandelions in a breeze. Grabbing his ankles with one hand, Leigh pulled a tissue from the box and wiped around the chubby folds of his legs and bum.

She lifted him into the metal sink, supporting his head in the awkward crook of her arm. It was lucky she was tall, I thought, because the tub was high and deep, and a shorter girl would have struggled to hold a slippery baby while scooping water over his head. As she lathered his fine blonde hair, the child began to fret, arching his back and smacking at the water with his fists. Leigh flinched as a dollop of suds hit her in the face but did not relinquish her grip. Blinking, she reached for the washer with one hand and gently dabbed the baby's eyes.

Again, the door opened and in strode an older woman with short grey hair. She grimaced at the sight of the five closed doors and the steam rising above them and, with a resigned shake of her head, came and stood by the wall with me.

'Been waiting long?'

I nodded. It had been a while. The baby was being pulled from the bath and wrapped in the towel on the mat.

'People take too long,' the old woman grumbled, hoisting at the crimplene strap of her swimmers and casting her eyes around the room. The baby turned and looked at her. She made a face at him. When he didn't react, she demanded his attention, loudly clicking her tongue.

'How old?' she asked, raising her voice above the hiss of the showers.

I saw Leigh pause and stiffen.

'Seven months,' she answered without looking around, her voice high and clear as a bell.

The old woman's eyes narrowed as she looked Leigh up and down, from her glossy ponytail to her cowrie anklet. If Leigh could sense the scrutiny, she gave no sign. She remained resolutely focused on her ministrations to the child, rubbing his skin with baby oil, patting him with powder, dabbing cream on the insect bite, checking his fingernails. I watched, intrigued, as she leaned forward and nipped at his nails with her teeth, putting paid to any conjecture that she might be his big sister. Out of the bag came a clean nappy, already folded, a box of safety pins, another tiny singlet and a blue jumpsuit with feet.

The aqua door opened again and Vicki emerged in her brunch coat, her carroty hair hanging in damp ringlets. Quick as a flash, the grumpy old woman pushed past her and went in.

'What's she doing?' Vicki hissed. 'You were here first. Go bang on the door.'

'No!'

'I can't believe you're still waiting.' She looked incredulously at the other doors—green, maroon, orange, yellow—all of them firmly shut.

At the sound of Vicki's voice, Leigh Mathieson turned around. The baby was fully dressed now and she held him against her chest, one hand splayed on the back of his flossy head.

'You're Paul Mitchell's sister,' she said.

Vicki looked stunned.

'Is he here?' Leigh asked.

I looked at Vicki. She swallowed and shook her head.

I was bursting to give Leigh the details—to tell her that Paul was spending the summer on our cousins' farm near Dunedoo while he tried to decide whether to leave school at the end of the year or carry on to the HSC and study Agriculture—but Vicki's silence warned me off.

Leigh nodded and I thought that she seemed a bit disappointed. She bent down and clipped the baby into the seat of the stroller and then turned her attention to the packing up: the bottles and lotions, the padded mat, the little lemon hair brush. She kicked the brake and wheeled the stroller around to face the door. Then she stopped and spoke to us again.

'Would you tell him Leigh Mathieson says hello?'

Again, Vicki said nothing. Leigh's gaze was cool and steady. There was no clock but you could hear the seconds ticking by.

'We'll tell him,' I blurted.

'Thank you,' said Leigh and we watched her leave, backwards, as she had come in, pulling the bulky stroller after her.

It was almost dark when Vicki and I passed the surfie vans again. A girl was crouched next to one lighting a gas lamp. We headed up the hill, through the powered sites and smells of dinners cooking. Little kids were still running around. Mothers were calling them.

'I don't think Paul was even her friend,' Vicki said suddenly. 'Why would she say hello to him? He'll think that's really weird.'

'We'll tell him, but.'

Vicki shrugged and quickened her pace. I hurried after her, stumbling in my thongs.

'Won't we, Vicki?'

'Won't we what?'

'Tell him.'

'I dunno.'

'We said we would.'

'You did.'

'I think we should.'

'Why's that?'

In a nearby caravan, a television burbled and I could smell sausages cooking on the stove. Why indeed. Why did it matter? Why did I feel so flustered? I cast around for an answer but found I didn't know.

Chopping Wood
K W George

Highly Commended

When he entered the low-roofed kitchen, the woman was peeling potatoes. She worked at the window in the light of the pewter-coloured sky, the old dog lying at her feet.

'Nothing I do makes him happy,' the boy blurted out.

She shook her head, murmuring something. He had to strain to hear her. She'd always spoken softly. Sometimes he wished she'd shout, just so that he knew she could.

'But why can't I do anything right?'

'It isn't you, love. It's his arthritis making him cranky. He's old and tired. We're both old and tired.' The peeler scraped against the potato flesh.

'But every time I do stuff for him he loses it. Every time. I'm sick of it.'

The boy walked across to the table where engine parts lay on newspaper like oily lumps of anthracite. He touched some, turned others. 'Alternator,' he muttered.

He was eighteen and had been helping his grandfather since he was ten and ought to know what a frigging alternator looked like by now, but he wasn't interested, didn't care—hadn't been for years. He picked up a bit in his hands and peered at it as if the greasy metal could tell him its name.

'Nan,' he called out, 'would you know an alternator if you met one?'

He crossed the room, holding a part in each hand.

'Which one, do you think?'

She shifted her weight and light from the window illuminated the pain in her eyes. It was her hip. She needed a new one, but hip replacements were expensive and big operations carried risks. Plus, his grandfather was scared. Sometimes the boy wondered what would become of the old guy if she died first. He was a cranky old sod now, imagine what he'd be like without her. He knew what he'd do if she went—he'd go, get the hell out.

She touched a part with the peeler. 'This one, maybe?'

The boy rested the metal on the sink's edge and stared out of the window. The shrubbery was just a shadowy blur. Sometimes he saw faces in the leaves, the way he saw them in clouds when he stared long and hard.

'Nan, there's something I want to tell you—'

'Put that thought out of your mind.'

'But you don't know what I'm going to say!'

'I do. You're going to tell me you want to move out, even though you don't have the money. I'm sorry but you're stuck with us for the moment. Can you understand that?'

The boy put the engine bits down amidst the tea-stained mugs and the dark red beets waiting to be rinsed. 'That's not what I was—'

'How far are you?' She was distracting him, but he went along with it because he loved her.

'Once I give him the alternator we're nearly done. It all has to be put back together of course, but that won't take long. Nan, I want to change courses.'

'What?' she said faintly. She dropped the potatoes one-by-one into the pot and held the metal to her chest like armour, guarding herself against his words, limping to the stove.

'I want to be a doctor.'

Pushing the container onto the gas, she lit the flame, bending to adjust the heat, one hand on her afflicted hip, and still she said nothing.

'Did you hear what I said?'

'And this change of heart,' she asked, drying her hands on her worn apron, 'when did that happen?'

'When I went with Rebecca to visit her friend.'

'Sophie?'

'I've never been in a hospital before. It sounds lame but I just know that's what I want to do. I never wanted to be an engineer, you know that.'

'But love, it'll break his heart.'

She pushed the grey curls from her lined face with the back of her hand. 'And where'll the money—'

'Money? What money?' His grandfather's voice in the doorway startled them both. With his beaked nose, thinning white hair, and khaki overalls ending several inches above his ankles, he was like an ancient eagle. Impervious and fierce.

'The money I owe her from yesterday,' the boy said, careful not to glance at the woman.

'You lending him money again? How much this time? You're not to lend him money, do you hear? He's got to make do.'

'I know,' the woman said.

'Well, if you know, why do you do it?'

The man's gaze fell on the engine parts on the sink. 'What are those doing there? If you've gone and got water on them ...' He pushed his glasses up his nose with two fingers and glanced at the boy. 'Where's the alternator? I ask you for one thing ...'

The boy crossed his arms and studied the slate floor. Its indentations, humps and crevices were like a landscape, another world, waiting to be explored ... Another life.

'You chopped that firewood yet?'

The boy didn't answer.

'No, I thought not,' his grandfather said. 'Get off your arse, then. Go on.'

Outside in the gloom, the cat sat to attention on the stump. The boy fondled her ears, then reached for the axe.

'Scat,' he said gently, and the cat raised herself, pushed out her white-socked front paws and arched her back in the damp air. Hopping down, she faded into the shadows.

The woodpile was in the lee of a corrugated iron shed, under a lean-to that staggered drunkenly over the sandy earth. The cat caught mice here, abandoning their bloodied corpses like sacrificial lambs. Tossing half a dozen blocks towards the stump, the boy hefted a piece and let its heaviness weigh down his palm. The chunk was cumbersome, the colour of rust threaded with veins. He positioned it on the stump, planted his feet apart, lifted the axe above his head and swung it down with a grunt. The wood splintered. Picking up a piece he repeated the act, and as the offcuts became narrower he steadied them with two fingers to hack at them, every so often gathering the fallen kindling and turfing it into an old cardboard box.

The kitchen light came on in the house and a soft glow coated the backyard, making the boy glance up. His grandfather was propped against the counter, one hand tucked under his armpit, the other scratching at his lowered temple. The murmur of voices reached the boy through the open window. She'd be telling him, which'd be a good thing. The old guy could have an apoplexy and then they could all move on ... with nothing changed ...

The boy sighed and gazed into the trees. Tendrils of light crawled across the ground into the long spikey grass and up the papery trunks. Sometimes he saw his mother's face here, but she'd been gone so long it was hard to remember what she looked like. Sometimes he saw a man who might be his father. Occasionally he saw his future, exotic and remote from here, but tonight only shadows shifted in the trees and in the patchwork of paddocks beyond.

He placed his left hand down on the stump and spread his fingers. Against his palm were sharp splinters and the wood's warm cushioning. He jiggled his hand, adjusting the axe's weight in the other, sliding the smooth handle backwards and forwards and backwards and forwards and then he swung the axe up and paused with it suspended in the air—

—Sharp and desperate, his grandfather's shout came from the house and the boy dropped the tool and ran.

In the kitchen, his grandmother lay on the floor with the old man on his knees beside her. The old guy was staring into her face, calling her name. He raised his head, said: 'do something!'

The boy dropped to the floor. He leaned forward and took his grandmother's hand. 'Move,' he instructed. The old man spluttered with indignation but the boy cut him off. 'Do you want me to do something or not?'

He couldn't find a pulse. Couldn't locate one in her wrist or at the base of her neck—

'Call an ambulance. Now!' he said, when the man didn't budge. And after the old man had heaved himself to his feet the boy reached across and pulled the woman's dress down from where it had been rucked up beyond her bony knees.

The phone was in the hallway. The boy heard the dial being repeatedly pulled back and released and listened to his grandfather's voice, gruff and yet oddly hesitant, and knew that it'd take at least thirty minutes for the medics to arrive from town.

Repositioning himself, he bent over the body. With two hands flat to the woman's chest, he pressed down and pumped and then he leaned forward to blow into her mouth and at some point he became aware that the old man had returned to kneel at her side. It looked to the boy as if the old guy were praying, but his grandfather wasn't a man who invested in God.

'It's okay, mate,' one of the medics said gently, pulling the boy away. 'We're here now. You can stop.'

His grandmother's arm was flung across the floor, the pale vulnerable underside exposed, the hand grasping at nothing. Her wedding ring was a thin glint of gold in the light and then the fingers twitched and the boy wanted to bawl his eyes out. He stuffed his fist into his mouth and bit back the tears, concentrated on the medics and their routine.

'You did good,' one said.

They lifted her onto the trolley and wheeled it out through the interleading door to the garage, murmuring something about tests, and hospital, but the details didn't matter. The boy knew where it was.

Alone on his knees, through blurred eyes, he saw the dog quivering under the table, the animal lost without her mistress.

'Missy?' he called gently. She heaved herself to her feet and came to him and, burying his face in her fur, inhaling her dogginess, he sobbed as if his heart were shattered.

He found his grandfather in the driveway, gazing after the receding lights of the ambulance as it bumped along the pot-holed dirt road back to town.

The boy sniffed. He held out the car keys. 'D'you want me to drive?'

His grandfather said nothing. He shambled across the yard and heaved himself into the passenger seat of the Land Cruiser.

'Close the door,' the boy told him, then reached across to do so. He held out the seatbelt. 'Here,' he said patiently, 'you need to put this on.'

They rattled across the cattle grid and trundled past rows of dark alfalfa that reached out to the darkness. The sky, stretched tight and taut above them, was like an animal skin tacked out to cure.

The old man muttered something.

'What?' The boy shifted the gearstick.

'Your father was a doctor.'

'What did you say?'

'I said, your father was a doctor.'

'My father—?'

'Yes.'

'But why did you not tell me … *before*?'

The silhouette of a passing telephone pole loomed like a crucifix as the old man gazed out of the window into the shadowy night. His shoulders were slumped and he seemed altogether insubstantial, as if he were a scarecrow and not a man.

'It's a long story,' he said at last.

'That's okay,' the boy told him, 'we've got time on our hands.'

The dusk seeped away. The lights on the dashboard glowed. The vehicle coasted along the road trailing a long banner of dust behind it, and the old man began to talk.

Scissor Tango

J.Anne DeStaic

Highly Commended

The hills at the edge of the city are burning. Ash of houses and trees and those small animals too slow in their escape, fill the air with grit and menace. The smell is so strong it drives the Vella twins inside despite the heat, despite the risk their mother will smell the joint they are smoking. They sit on the floor of the dressing room watching her through the glass door as she fusses over Mr. Clive, their dance teacher. Her image distorts in the door's old glass.

'She could kiss his prick from there.'

'Oh, gross, April. Don't say that.'

'Why not? It's true. Look.'

May looks. Their mother kneels very close in front of him her forehead almost brushing his thigh as she smoothes the zip sewn in the side of his pants. In the soft dull light from the lamp on the table it is hard to see exactly where her fingers press then pinch the fabric to add a pin.

April hands May the joint, now just a tiny stub. It burns her fingers as she sucks, and she coughs and April presses her hand over her twin's mouth, dragging her out the door to the verandah that runs the length of the house. They collapse on the lumpy timber slats their backs against the wall, legs stretched out, feet pointed, the lazy, pale smoke between them.

Mr. Clive is having a ballroom costume made—high-waisted elegant pants, a close cut shirt and a pink cummerbund to match his partner's dress that hangs on the rack behind him. Their mother fusses now with his jacket, making him wear it inside out so she can tack the lining close and correctly to his fattening frame. May gives April the stub but there is nothing left. She flicks the ember onto the lawn. For a moment she thinks she sees rain starting to fall. She stretches her foot out past the roof's overhang, but there is no rain.

Their mother's voice cracks through the window.

'Girls, where are you? Come in now.'

They don't move. April whispers:

'If she marries him, I'll kill him. And her. I mean it.'

'I know where you are. Get a move on. Miss Cilla is here and she wants to see the red tutus.'

They stand and start giggling because it all seems so funny in the dark heat with mosquitoes whining and biting and cars splashing them with yellowed light as they drive slowly over the speed bump on the road in front of their house. The girls walk inside chewing gum. April always has gum in her pocket. She chews with her mouth open.

'For heaven's sake, girls, we don't have all day. You know where they are? In the sewing room. Off you go and don't forget the tights and shoes in the boxes on the shelves.'

The three adults—Mr.Clive, his sister Miss Cilla, and their mother—are in the fitting room and the door between the sewing and fitting rooms is heavy old glass with a long crack in one corner. Once it is closed the heat is horrible, the air heavy, and the twins sweat. They hear the tiny crack of the seal breaking as their mother unscrews a bottle of wine. April turns the light on. Now they can see Mr. Clive. He watches them, sips his wine, leans against the wall in his tight waltz pants and his white shirt. May moves away so his eyes can't reach her. She pulls the tights up her sweaty legs then steps into the red tutu with its scratchy frills, easing it up over tights and over her flesh. She ties on the red pointe shoes, then flexes her feet, driving their points into the carpet, arching bones, cracking joints.

April stands in front of the glass door, tights on. She moves the tutu up slowly, knowing that he watches as the red fabric conceals belly, then ribs, then her small round breasts. She snaps the ribbon straps in place and stands there red in the electric light. The joint makes her heart beat slowly. And slowly she turns away from the door and faces her twin. They straighten their shoulder straps, smooth the scoop-shaped neck of the bodice and fluff up the skirts. And if this was a performance, they would take colours from sticky pots of eye shadow, smother the foam ends of the applicators and paint eyelids, fix false eyelashes in place, outline lips, fill them in. They had no need for mirrors. They look exactly the same.

Their mother opens the door.

'Come on girls. Now!'

In the fitting room, in front of her mother and Clive and Cilla, May stands en pointe, turns slowly, arms en couronne while her mother straightens and fusses at the fabric that doesn't need straightening or fussing. Miss Cilla walks around May.

'Looks good Mrs. Vella. I have never dressed my girls in red before but the drama I think will work very well. The music's Piazolla. A tango—very sharp.'

April stands very still. May sees her reflection in the long mirror that leans against the far wall. Mr. Clive is beside her with his arm behind her. And doing what? May can't tell. But he stops when he sees her watching and moves his hand up to April's shoulder. He says:

'You girls look great. Very grown up.'

Their mother preens.

'Okay. Off you go and be careful getting out of the tights. It wasn't easy getting enough of the same colour. There aren't any spares. Clive, just leave the waltz on the chair there. I'll finish it tomorrow.'

Miss Cilla and their mother take the wine bottle and glasses and leave the fitting room. The twins go next door and wait in the dark till Mr. Clive is changed and they hear him leave.

April is *en pointe*. She sticks her bum out, makes her arms ugly.

'Look at me Miss Cilla. Look at me. God, May, you're an arselick sometimes.'

They change without speaking and the smoking and the verandah and the car headlights racing over them seem so long ago and they will never be friends again. Never. April goes back into the fitting room. May hangs up her own tutu, picks up April's from the floor and hangs it next to hers. She fold the tights, puts them back in their boxes, tucks the beautiful red ribbons into their pointe shoes and puts them on the shelf.

April comes back. She has their mother's shears in one hand, opening the blades, then snapping them shut with a cruel metal crunch. Mr. Clive's pants are in her other hand the perfect outline of his bulky shape.

'Maysie. What do you reckon?'

She smiles. She slices the pants from the waist down to the crotch, turns the garment and slices back up, a wedge now cut from the front. She holds the pants against herself and pokes the shears upward through the hole and waves them around like a sharp and hard steel penis.

'Shit, what have you done?'

The pants drop to the floor. The scissor blades are open and April slides one blade down her forearm, quick, vertical. The skin unzips, folds out, red liquid beads popping down the edges of the cut then running together like a river. May can see shiny, slippery tissue, almost grey in colour, at the bottom of the slice.

'Oh shit. I didn't mean …'

April drops the shears. The tips of the blades jam into the carpet and the floorboard underneath and wobble. April holds her arm against her chest, her eyes are wide and she looks for a moment as if she has won a prize and can't believe it and then her face creases.

'Shit. Shit. It hurts.'

'I'll get Mum.'

'No. No. May. It'll be okay. It's not that bad.'

But it is bad. May grabs the first aid bag from the shelf in the cutting room scattering paper patterns and lengths of soft pink chiffon. She wraps and re wraps her sister's arm while blood seeps through the first and then the second bandage and there are no more.

'You have to go to hospital. April. I'm getting Mum, April. I have to.'

April sniffs hard and stops crying, gripping, bruising May's arm with her good hand.

'You can drive May. I know you can. You can take me to the hospital and we'll tell her after its all sorted.'

'Shit, April, I haven't got my P-plates or anything.'

'Fuck you May. If we tell her now then Mr. Clive will see what I did to his pants.'

Suddenly, terribly, May doesn't want Mr. Clive anywhere near her and the fear of him is so great and so strange that she takes the car keys and her mother's wallet from her bag on the kitchen table and drives her sister to the hospital and it is nine o'clock on a Friday night and the traffic is slow and April lies in the back seat hugging her arm to her chest, rocking and crying and May thinks her twin will die and every light—every single one of them—is red and she is in the wrong lane to turn right and they have to drive on and double back and she hates this city and all its people and all its cars. She wishes the fire with all its fury in the hills surrounding, would break free of its containment lines, come down and consume them all.

May sees how they look at April at the hospital—the stud in her nose, the ring in her eyebrow. She sees how they look at her, at May, with her neat words and neat ponytail, her plain clothes, her plain skin. The nurse said it was amazing how much they were alike. Except as she walked away and pulled the curtain around April lying on her bed, the word that she used was 'weird'. Weird how much they were alike.

And not.

A doctor sews her up–not so much blood after all and not so deep, he says. They give her a letter and tell May to get her home and give her Codeine or Panadol. They say seven days for the stitches. But May knows this because April needed stitches for a cut on her leg just six months before. Back then, they had sat in a queue for three hours to get those stitches out. This time, April whispers she will do it herself. Her mother is a dressmaker after all. She knows how to cut thread.

On the way home it rains, hard and heavy like bullets hitting the car. May drives as slowly as she can while all around her, cars honk and drivers gesture.

At home, their mother is in the cutting room, black stretch satin on the table, paper patterns weighted over its length. A bottle of vodka is on the table and her music is loud, drowning the quiet noise of the girls opening the front door, climbing the stairs to their bedroom. The pants will be finished by the morning and Mr. Clive will never know.

The Red Tango Troupe from The Lombard Academy will be a huge success this season, but without April, the scar on her arm too red and too obvious to hide.

White Water Glimpses

David Brewster

Commended

In one of their photo albums, crushed in the boot along with the other miscellaneous life treasures she had grabbed, there is a photo of her on this hill above the old racetrack. It must be from the late '60s—hair free, channelling Jean Shrimpton in a white, above-the-knee slip. Like her wedding dress, she had sewn it on her mother's Singer which had been bequeathed as a present when she married John. That was probably the last time she'd felt its exciting bite between her fingers, reimagining the frock from the scandalised stories in the *Sydney Morning Herald*. John had been unusually silent in the face of the approving comments from their overdressed friends, the first turns of a reel winding in attributes that once had been appealing.

In the image she is laughing at someone off camera; the mounting yard is in the background.

'A grey!' she had delighted at the marshalling of the maiden plate.

The SPs, late middle-aged replicants with shabby cream-coloured short-sleeved business shirts, clutching cigarettes and wads of paper, had sneered at her choice with long odds.

'Did you know they tried to breed the grey thoroughbreds out,' she'd asked rhetorically, showing the slip proudly to her new husband. 'On the basis of genetic inferiority.'

Preoccupied, trying to get the bar girl's attention, he had responded over his shoulder, 'You'll be first at being last.'

A few years later she had won what felt like a small fortune on *Silver Knight* in the Melbourne Cup. Hopes of putting the winnings towards a cruise with her recently widowed mother went unrealised. John had insisted on a boat of another kind—a cuddy cabin with an oversized outboard.

'When we have some boys, I'll take them out,' was the challenge masquerading as an ex-post explanation he provided the day it unexpectedly appeared as a squatter in the garage. Two daughters interested in land sports eventually put paid to that idea. The elder had only last year popped back from overseas to sell the virgin hulk on e-Bay for a meagre sum, in one of her sporadic efforts to 'sort the house out.'

The track today looks like a different photograph: one of the brittle images she recalls seeing at her grandparents', the silver oxide decomposing, a metallic fog across the surface, obscuring the funereal clothing and faces of the long dead. The smoke is thicker than ever in the past week. People stand, agitated, in small groups. There is nowhere to sit except on the hill, where the haze seems worse, or so John complains. They seem to have arrived later to the evacuation centre than most people, their stay and fight plans in disarray after his unexplained change of heart. She checks her phone. There is still no connection. The battery is already half gone, and they have no spare charger. John had baulked at the price tag in Betta Electrical. Told her he'd give her the equivalent in cash if she remembered to plug her devices in at night for a month.

Rumours abound, overheard from nearby congregations or at the RFS tent where high school kids are dispensing water bottles. Malua Bay is gone. The wind's changed, we may need to relocate towards Bega. To stem the bile from her gnawing stomach she stitches together odd fortunes: that John had refused her suggestion that he could do with a dog in his life; the Cotoneasters he had insisted on planting as a border screen fifty years ago might finally have met their match. It is nearly midnight on New Year's Eve. The yawning uncertainty of another year stretches ahead, the days more obscured than ever. The air is still baking hot but she feels in need of a jumper. If the house is gone, will there be any foundation left?

Deceptively languid, the Murray slides under the patterned shadows of the river gums. As a girl from the coast she had always found the colours of the inland waterways distasteful, like the gloomy palette of coarse fabrics in the window of an army disposal shop. Walking the banks, in her 60-minute exercise allotment, the last month she has come to accept a beauty in the landscape, albeit one tempered by her constant juxtaposition of an imagined vista where the native flora has not been stripped for farming. Far away, where the bulldozed remains of their home are being carted away by state government contractors, the dead forests sweep down from the ranges, unbroken to the sea.

She is loath to return to the motel but it is lunchtime; with the lockdown there is nowhere else to eat. Evicted from the now closed holiday park, their caravan sits in the deserted street, accumulating debris from scrappy hakeas. Another impulse purchase, executed at the ambitiously named holiday home dealership in Wollongong the day after a 36-hour exodus from the south. At the time, John's logic had seemed reasonably sound—insurance claims, demolition, council approvals, and a shortage of labour, would mean a year or more before any reconstruction. Not that her consent had been sought, but she'd nodded anyway. At that point, all she had wanted was a shower and to sleep horizontally.

Outside the door, their six-cylinder sedan still seems to exude the painful cries that left her stressed for hours after each progressive move west on their stalled circumnavigation of the country. At their last stop in Echuca they had settled into what was becoming a familiar routine: John, cursing her jerky efforts to navigate the van onto the levelling chocks without crushing his hands; awning up; porta-chairs out; reserved nods from neighbouring sites, which would turn to uncomfortably familiar bonhomie that evening after Chardonnay on the terrace of the communal kitchen facility.

She misses the University of the Third Age classes she used to deliver to an unpredictable conglomerate of seniors, sea-changers and the voluntarily unemployed.

'I don't know how you found the time,' Jan from the site, two down, had said as, reaching for the hummus, she knocked their wine onto the bull ants below. Those days had seemed endless, from the early morning crepitation of full bladders padding past on the gravel, to the final delivery to darkness as the blinding roo-shooters, inevitably employed by a short-stay visitor, clicked off for the night.

'That Jan is a twit,' had been her husband's contribution to the day, after he saw them sharing tea before leaving her alone again to go fishing.

At the wharf museum, they'd stared at the illuminated map of the east coast river system. Their clothes, floral polyester prints from Kmart, were inadequate against an early autumn breeze; hers bought in desperation in the Illawarra, Jan's apparently a wardrobe staple. She had watched with a creeping horror as red lights tracked the incremental expansion of the paddleboat network into the country's interior.

'Talk about an invasive species,' she'd commented eventually, 'that in less than a generation of the First Fleet, we'd penetrated so far inland.'

Jan had reserved her response until they stood outside overlooking the river loitering below.

'I think a person needs to look forward. You can't change the past.'

It had not been the skeletal remains of their house that most shocked her. That unveiling had involved little more than the disappointingly familiar feeling of visiting a tourist site viewed many times beforehand on the internet. Rather, the scorched and still glowing hillsides that stretched into the haze had lashed her, viscerally, almost physically. In the morning sun, the contours and ridgelines, once a soft wink behind canopy and understorey, lay sharp, exposed, awful and unwanted in their clarity, like a parent seen naked for the first time in decades.

'It felt like something in my DNA broke,' she had confessed to Jan the night before they were forced from the park. 'That the land was part of me and that part was dead.' She'd had too much to drink, their move the next day to a motor lodge they could scarcely afford necessitating prophylactic sedation. 'I mean I've always understood there was a connection between Aboriginal people and their country but for the first time in my life I caught a glimpse of what that really meant. I felt what it meant. I'm so ashamed that was what it took to make me understand.'

Jan had patted her hand, to a frown from John at the next table.

'Joyce, what's done is done.' She had excused herself to sit under the inadequate flouros in the toilet block and cry in a cubicle. Jan meant no harm. Perhaps at this point in life being well-intentioned was the best she could hope for.

Outside the motel it has been raining now for three days. Sitting at the window, watching hydrangeas that remain thirsty beneath overly protective eaves, she rues the conversion of this thwarted salvation into such torture. It plays on her mind in an eternal loop, like the cheap local ads on the television, which blares in their small room 16 hours a day. Later, lingering in the local Coles, she irrelevantly compares nutritional panels between expensive and house brand goods. On Thursdays and Fridays, a part-time lady at the in-store bakery is usually up for a chat towards the end of her day.

'I asked for more shifts,' the woman says from behind her mask in an unexpectedly erudite conversation. 'It's busy enough, and anything to get me away from Frank. You can't change people's orbits at our age without a major collision.'

Her younger daughter is a fount of exasperation, like the pointless inground sprinkler system that, inexplicably, still waters their neighbour's barren block.

'I can't believe you're selling now. It's the worst possible time. And there are sea views again.'

The vista is one of the many backdrops against which she has erected mental barriers since their return. She refuses to delight in any aspect of the destruction, appalled by her offspring's opportunism.

'Why would you wait until you are 70 to live on your own?' comes the frustrated voice of the other daughter over a stalled FaceTime image on her phone. 'Sarah and myself can't look after you.'

'I,' she corrects, instinctively, conclusively, tired of the dressage of threats presented as observations. Above, cockatoos wheel and scream in a great, hungry flock. They gather in masses amongst the denuded lignotubers and desperately rend at the epicormic buds, tearing into the fragile efforts at revival.

Jan had hugged her the night before the travel restrictions were lifted and they'd fled to their respective safe havens. Or, in their case, to the backyard of their youngest daughter and her sullen de-facto's uninspiring brick three-bedroom, in a windless new inland development on the Central Coast. Unaccustomed to such spontaneous intimacy, she had stiffened awkwardly before overcompensating and patting Jan's shoulder like a nostalgic pet owner.

Jan had gone to say something, her mouth moving silently, as if dancing over forgotten words in the lead up to a chorus, before saying crisply, 'Sarah is going to be so thrilled to see you and John again.'

To her children, one impatiently waiting to get back in the car, the other in a distant land itself ravaged by fires, she says eventually, 'Did you know that this is Yuin country? Imagine, living here my whole life, and only just finding that out. I've offered to run a course on local history, instead of the Italian.'

The spinning wheel, mirroring the melodramatic eye roll of her youngest, is silent before issuing a diagnosis.

'Mum, I think you might be having a breakdown. They say lots of people are.'

She turns to the whitecaps, visible beyond the fence line of blackened casuarinas.

'No,' she responds with a wave of her index finger to the red telephone symbol. 'Just listening.'

With Eyes To See

Eleanor Ratcliffe

Commended

Vladimir walked in the door and the children had just finished their early dinner. Alexei, as always, rushed over; Anna was reading her book and only came over when Alexei gasped. This disappointed Vladimir a little, though he knew he should have expected it, for it was Anna who had wanted a puppy to begin with.

'Anna, come look!' said Alexei, probably not for the first time that day. He was ten, in the final year before that boyish excitement would give way to a practised nonchalance. Anna, even at twelve, could discern true novelties from Alexei's usual attention-seeking. And there it was: a little dog, a girl, with straight, pointed ears and a white stripe down the bridge of her face.

'Anna!' he exclaimed again, but she was already there behind him, crouching to meet the pup at eye level.

'Papa!' she said, and beamed at him, 'She is perfect.' And for a short moment Vladimir allowed himself the feeling of being self-satisfied, even though he'd questioned himself as he brought the little creature home. For a brief moment, he saw a snatch of Anna once again as a little girl, when her capacity for joy could be ignited by as little as new buttons on an old coat.

Anna knew it would be silly to ask what breed the dog was when it was so clearly a mongrel, albeit one who had been washed and fed, not at all like those who she saw strolling the streets of Leningrad. And anyway, nobody she knew had a dog of any particular breed.

Alexei was immune to the dog's clear lack of education.

'Sit!' he commanded so incessantly that it began to sound more like a bark more than any noise the dog herself was making. The little dog herself just spun around wagging her tail with delight and made a survey of the room by sniffing its perimeter diligently.

Anna preferred to observe. She noticed when the dog had made her way back to its starting point in the corner of the room, and approached calmly. Then she held out her wrist as an offering. The little dog licked Anna's fingers before calmly submitting to patient, gentle strokes of her back.

'She's perfect,' Anna said again, then quietly, 'how did you know I wanted a dog?'

He decided to indulge her belief in her own discretion, instead of pointing out that her attempts to hide her desperate wish had not been so well hidden. He would tell himself this was so as not to embarrass her, though it was just as much to shield himself from thoughts of all the other things he knew she must have desired but kept secret, for knowing that her father could never provide them.

Vladimir opened the brown bag he'd brought home with him and proudly showed all the accoutrements that came with the little dog. A little ball, which she plainly recognised and raced for as soon as it was produced; a half-chewed slipper; a length of rope fashioned into a leash; and an enamel bowl to fill with water.

'What about a collar?' Alexei asked, 'I want to get a little tag for her to wear on her neck with a name on it, so everyone knows she's mine.'

'Ours,' Anna corrected.

'Ours.'

Vladimir opened his mouth, and hesitated, but said nothing.

'Anyway, it doesn't matter,' said Anna quickly and threw the ball. 'She knows us already. Dogs are very good at knowing how to come home.'

'How would you know when we've never had one?' said Alexei, innocently, but Anna looked wounded.

'I read about it in a book,' she said quietly.

'And it's true, too, and a very good way to learn things,' Vladimir added quickly.

'And what about a little bed for her?' asked Alexei, and Vladimir again looked awkward. The dog settled quietly into Anna's lap and closed her bright black eyes.

'She has a bed here,' Anna cooed softly, and ran her fingers through the dog's dark hair. Alexei tried to throw the ball again, but the little dog was close to sleep. She blinked lazily and began the deep restful breaths of peace.

'Good girl,' whispered Anna, and the tip of the little dog's tail quivered in acknowledgement.

Alexei began to chat excitedly of his grand plans for his new companion. Not only all the tricks he must train her in, of course, which began with sitting and staying but quickly gave way to wilder and more elaborate schemes of throwing and catching and somersaults. But then, too, the question of which friends she must be shown off to, and in what order? Starting from tomorrow, of course.

Alexei had many tiers of friends. It might seem intuitive to show them off his prize to those who were his oldest and best friends—but what of those to whom he wished to get to know better, with whom a little pup was the perfect way to curry favour? And what of those whom he knew especially loved dogs? What of Dmitri around the corner—a friend, yes, not his closest, but one who had a special understanding of dogs, who would see, better than others, this dog's unique intelligence, the kindness and patience in her wet eyes, the dignified proportion of her snout, how uniquely alert her ears were when standing to attention. Who, among all of his friends, could recognise that this was clearly a superior dog?

While Alexei chatted excitedly, Anna continued the meditative soft gentle strokes along the dog's back, half closing her eyes in bliss. She did not have the heart to tell Alexei that she could see the little dog had seen some kind of tumult in her mongrel street life before arriving here. She already knew Alexei's fanciful schemes would probably never come to fruition. She could see, just as clearly as Dmitri would, the kindness and circumspection in the little bitch's eyes. But she saw, too, an uneasiness, a trepidation, and this only intensified her drive to hold the little animal close, to reassure and cuddle calmly in the confines of this house.

Vladimir wondered at this. It was not that Anna didn't have any friends, exactly. It was that he always had the sense they didn't know how to truly see her, or were impressed by the same things that impressed her, even if those things were just a little dog from the streets. He could see the eyes that looked on the little dog in her lap with tenderness were not the same that looked on her friends at a birthday party, that they did not light up in the same way when chatting about the day's gossip on the way home from school. Did it hurt her to hear Alexei prattle on about his so very many 'friends,' even if she must know that so many of them were no more than the schoolyard company of boyhood? Anyway, Vladimir had to stop Alexei before he kept going.

'That's enough, Alexei,' he said, 'It was time for bed ten minutes ago.'

'But will I be able to take her to show Dmitri tomorrow morning, on the way to school?'

'Time for bed.'

'Good girl,' repeated Anna softly.

Vladimir waited until the children had both left for school the next morning before packing his briefcase and going to work. The little bitch looked up dolefully at him as he slipped the rope leash on her neck, and at once he saw both the sweetness in her eyes that was so obvious to Alexei, and the weariness glimpsed by Anna.

He walked to work. He figured the dog would enjoy it. When he arrived at the lab, he knew the others would roll their eyes at him, at how he was soft-hearted for thinking the dog would want to spend her last evening playing with his children.

But wasn't it the least he could do? He thought of the dogs he'd grown up with, much like this one, who couldn't talk but who knew when his mother was ill, seriously ill, or who slept at the end of his bed after a bad day at school?

They loaded the little dog into the space capsule and Vladimir wondered if her little half chewed slipper might go too, to comfort her, but he was too embarrassed to suggest it.

'Good girl,' he muttered softly instead, and again she wagged her tail just as she had in Anna's lap last night: a constrained little half-wag at the very tip of her tail, the expression of a street mutt who had learnt early that it was dangerous to give away too much, but for whom the thrill of being recognised was irresistible. Or simply an animal who had been trained to stay in a confined capsule. Maybe both.

Wasn't it the least he could do? he asked himself again.

The children would ask when they came home from school where their dog had gone. Well, Vladimir thought grimly, I suppose this will be their first experience of someone you love ominously and suddenly disappearing.

The rocket launched with an unearthly sound, like something biblical, and he looked away, realising that it had never occurred to him or any of the other researchers how much dogs hated loud noises like thunder or fireworks. Laika would be orbiting the Earth for a few days yet. Laika. That was what they called her in the lab. She would be put to sleep with a poison pill before she ran out of oxygen, the technician said, if all went to plan.

And what was it all for, anyway? To test the compatibility of space with life, yes, Vladimir knew intellectually, or more cynically, to parade the advancement of the Soviet technology, of course—but that wasn't what he meant.

As the craft barrelled towards the atmosphere and gradually slipped out of sight, Vladimir thought of Laika's bright black eyes. So many pairs of eyes across the world, and how few can ever claim to be the first to witness something truly unseen before? But it was Laika's eyes that were the first to ever gaze down on the Earth as a perfect orb, undivided by nations, riven only by the seas and continents the planet had made for herself; a symphony of blues and greens and sand and whiteness. Did the trembling little dog look out and feel the awe, even if the reason was beyond her understanding?

What a delicious cosmic joke, he thought, that for all the fanfare of progress and triumph, the very first eyes to behold something no other creature on Earth had ever seen, that would change history forever—those eyes belonged to a little street mutt, not a party official or president or a philosopher-king.

And as her eyes became the first ever to see that giant blue and green whole, giant and yet so tiny in the universe, he wondered if she would remember Alexei and Anna, and the fumbling love they'd showered on her final evening on Earth? Would she remember Vladimir himself, would she understand it was love, in his own roundabout, imperfect way, that had made him want to bring her to them, even if it was only for one night, before she left Earth forever?

'Good girl,' he said again, quietly.

Playing Hide And Seek

Lee Franklin

Commended

Three brothers sit silent in the hollow of a large boab tree. They are the best hiders ever, their mother tells them that all the time and there's no way they are ever going to find them. All they have to do is wait quietly and patiently for a signal from one of their mothers. Mandu, the oldest at five, feels the pressure of keeping the younger two safe from the devils on horseback. Gelar is a whole year younger, but resents Mandu telling him what to do all the time, thinks he should be in charge some times. The youngest, at two, is Kulan who finds it very hard to keep quiet at the best of times. Several times Mandu has to signal him to be quiet.

A bee flies in, lands on Kulan's nose. The boy looks at the bee, can see it looking back. He silently asks the bee not to sting. Mandu watches the bee on his brother's nose, gets annoyed that it just sits there. He swings his hand and squashes the bee. The sharp stinger penetrates the skin of Kulan's nose, but he doesn't cry out. He shuts his eyes and thinks about the kangaroo their uncle will bring home and cook on the fire. Thinks about the taste of its roasted flesh on his tongue and the full feeling in his belly. Already the area has turned red, makes Mandu feel bad that he squashed the bee, but there is nothing he can do but wait for one of their mothers to send them the signal.

After a while their legs get cramped in the small hollow, but still they don't move, don't make a sound. The devils on horseback may still be out there, trying to trick them into coming out of their hiding spot. But the brothers who are the best at hiding, refuse to give up, refuse to come out until they hear the signal. Until the devils have all gone far away.

With the setting sun, the brothers fall asleep in the hollow. Mandu dreams about the time they caught a goanna and took it back to camp in the old kerosene tin and how the mothers were so proud of them catching their own food. Gelar is dreaming about the story of the rainbow serpent Wagyl he has heard around the campfire at night. When they wake up there is no light left.

They aren't sure how long they have been in the tree hollow, but they know it is far too long. The mothers should have sent the signal long before now.

Kulan gets scared and starts to cry. Gelar tries to be brave, tries very hard not to cry. Mandu has to get angry to get the toddler to stop crying so he can listen for tell-tale sounds of the devils. There is nothing but the sounds of birds roosting in the upper branches of the tree, but still he is anxious.

The bellies of the brothers call out in hunger and it eventually drives them from their hiding spot. Slowly, cautiously they make their way home. They step slowly through the bush, stop often to listen, but can hear no human sounds.

They reach the clearing that has been their home, expecting to feel mother's arms around them and uncles laughing with relief. But the camp is empty and the fire cold. There is no kangaroo roasting in flames, no uncle to chastise them for staying away too long, no mothers to hold them to her chest. It is dark and empty and it scares them. Kulan starts to cry again, but this time Mandu wants to cry as well. Doesn't tell his brother to stop crying, or be a man. Gelar sits by the fire as if it is still blazing and can warm him up. He wants someone to tell him what to do next. Wants the family to appear out of the darkness, explain they were out hunting. He wants his uncles to light the fire and throw a kangaroo on the flames, watch over it while they tell the brothers stories of the dream time. But none of that happens and he can feel the other two looking to him for answers he doesn't have.

They enter the small tin hut one of their uncles made out of scrap he picked up from the edges of a town nearby. It too is cold and empty. All of the few possessions their family had are gone. All that is left is the bare ground. The three brothers cling together, try to understand what has happened, where the family could have gone. They try not to think about the possibility that the devils on horseback took them away. The uncles always told them they weren't interested in them, only the three brothers, though they never said why.

It gets colder and the older brother goes off, gathers many small branches for them. Inside the tin hut, they lie down in the corner, spread the branches on top. They know it will help keep them warm during the night and prevent them from being found. Mandu tells the others that in the morning the family will find their way back, the mothers will be proud of how brave they were and they will all laugh about it.

When the sun rises and light returns to the tin hut, the brothers are woken by the noise of men and machinery. They look at each other. The noise is unfamiliar to them. Gelar thinks it must be the Wagyl come for them. But

Mandu hears the devils voices, tells the others it can't be the Wagyl, tells them it's the devils come back without their horses. They pull the branches over themselves, make sure they can't be seen. They don't speak, don't move, just wait for the devils to leave and the family to return. They are the best hiders ever, their mother tells them that all the time and there's no way they are ever going to find them.

A man gets down from the tractor, looks at the last ugly tin hut that is barely standing upright. He can still hear the screams of the women when they were forcibly removed the previous day. They called for sons, mere babies, though the soldiers were sure there were no children at the camp. The soldiers said they were talking nonsense as they dragged the frantic women away. Now there is just the clean up. All because some bloke wants to clear the land and give his cattle even more grazing land. Jumping back on the tractor, he steers it toward the shanty building. As the tin crumples under the tyres he thinks he can hear a small child crying.

The Storm

M McQuillen

I sat under my tree with Sean once. It was the only time he took lunch early so we could eat together. He came down to the park at eleven and we had falafels and a fruit platter and watched the ducklings. Back when this season's batch were fuzzy and palm-sized.

Sean told me he didn't like sitting under trees. Especially when the trunk leans over your picnic spot.

'Tree-related injuries are way more common than you'd think.'

Sean always worried about stuff like that.

When we took the train we never sat in the first or last carriage.

'But this is my tree,' I told him. 'I eat here every day.'

He knocked the trunk a few times with his palm.

'You shouldn't,' he said, 'there's like a thousand straighter trees in this park.'

So we shuffled round the trunk out of the shade, faced the city instead, and he was happy to stay and finish his watermelon.

When he left he said we'd spent too long in the midday sun. I watched him brushing dust off his bum until he was lost between the buildings.

Unless you count Sean, there was no warning. Yesterday I had my wonky tree and a lunch spot. Now the trunk has taken my seat and the tip is taking a dip. Are there casualties at the lake?

It's early. Hopefully the ducks are safe in bed.

Does this feel like shock? It doesn't feel like much at all. It's the same old tree if I tilt my head. The leaves are green. It just needs a hand getting back up. One of the gardeners should tie a rope round it and rev their ute up the path. Ideally before eleven.

At the cafe I spend the morning sweeping leaves and butts from the courtyard. Laying tea towels 'round the base of doors and drawing *please-don't-slip* signs with Sharpies.

'Didn't last long, I think, but the quick ones are intense.' My manager sets out breakfast croissants while I mop. 'Did you see the tree?'

'I didn't hear a storm last night.'

'Well you don't sleep here in the park, do ya?'

At lunch my tree is still down but now some tape is up. Right 'round every branch plus the big chunks of path the roots have raised. A council gardener is collecting the rubble and I ask how long it will take to get my tree back up. He laughs when he realises I'm not joking.

'About 20 years?'

The back of his truck sinks chunk by chunk and I hover to watch. There's a bed of dirt in the tray to keep each toss quiet.

My mind goes strange places when I don't eat lunch. Viewing angles from high up in office buildings. Phantom vibrations from non-calls.

By the time his tray's full my break is over.

The station near my cafe is underground. Giant escalators drop you off right where the driver's cab pulls up. For the first time in months I walk halfway down the platform.

These days I get the three-thirty. When the train finds daylight I dig out late lunch and take one bite.

Next morning, some branches are gone. The smell of sawdust is a clue. Not that I need one, I can see the sawdust. One time, I pulled a houseplant out of its pot and the leaves wilted straight away. But there are leaves here that still haven't heard the news.

When I'm on the counter, a tourist points through our kitchen wall.

'What happen?'

I think he's German. He has a yellow jacket and a big family.

'It fell over,' I tell him.

Then I make six teas.

Tourists love our park. It's right next to the city. There's no other reason why. At lunch I sit on the lawn and watch them buzz around the trunk-hole. Trees must stay up where they're from. A young guy with a European beard climbs under the tape for root selfies.

It's not the first fallen tree I've seen up close. We found one on a bush walk. Eucalyptus trunks aren't so slender when they're sideways at eye level.

Sean yelled when I moved to cut around it.

'Never climb through the hole from a fallen tree!'

He grabbed my arm to save me from myself.

'Sometimes fallen trees right themselves,' he told me. 'Without warning! People have been crushed to death.'

He gave me a boost and I flipped over the trunk, fresh bark-rash on my stomach. Then he jumped too quick behind me and lost his legs.

'Glad we took the safe route,' I laughed.

He was fine. Just muddy.

When we pressed on I pressed him. How could a fallen tree possibly right itself?

'I dunno,' he said, 'but plenty of people have been killed by shit they don't understand.'

Sean worked in insurance. Does that make sense? He probably still does. If I ever forget where, I just need to check the skyline.

My mind goes strange places when I don't eat lunch. Why do big buildings never just fall? The city must have hundreds. What are the odds?

Sean probably could have told me.

His building is near the big department stores. That's where I went on Fridays until he finished. Testing out couches in fake apartments. Reading book after book with my feet up. Checking my phone at the bottom of each page. Wondering if I'd ever be moved along.

To be clear, I hope his building stays up. But I wouldn't complain if it was twenty metres shorter.

We only *sat* under my tree once. But another time we stood. He finished work after seven and I finished a novel lying on a brown chaise that would have looked nicer in a corner. It was dark but not cold and we didn't want the noodles we'd half-planned. So we took a walk in the park, ended up back at my tree.

There was no safety chat that time. Perhaps he felt better standing up. Ready to leap us out of danger if it toppled.

If he hadn't pressed me so hard to the trunk my tree might have had one more storm in it.

That tourist is still behind the tape, up to his waist, inspecting my tree upturned root by root. His top half is laughing and shouting and motioning for others to join him. He annoys me, but that's not why I don't warn him. I don't warn him because what would be the point?

When does something wrong ever really just right itself?

Next morning there's nothing left but the taped off hole. Not even a dint in my lunch spot. And what does a tree weigh? Ten elephants? A thousand?

Someone orders a toasted ham and cheese sandwich and I start crying right as the heat light flicks red to green.

'It's nothing,' I tell the manager. And then I tell her the truth:

'It's about the tree.'

'Uh-huh,' she says.

By lunch even the hole is gone. Covered with a turf quilt. They must keep little grass squares somewhere. Growing in the lab, waiting for parks to need skin grafts. The tape is gone too, but the patches need to heal so I keep my distance.

It takes a drifting lap of the park to confirm what I already knew. All the other good spots are taken.

There's a wedding shoot and I stare too long. The groom's eyes flick at me right as the flash goes off. They're on the tree-lined path down the middle of the park. That's where everyone gets their snaps done. It's all even-spaced and even-height and dead straight. No trees missing here. But there are still signs of damage if you look for them. Branches with fresh jagged wounds dragged far off into the bushes. A small tear in the rotunda's roof.

Sean told me never to leave the cafe in a storm. It's not just about falling branches. He said that under trees is the second most dangerous place to be when there's lightning. Thankfully I don't like eating wet sandwiches.

It rains overnight and already the seams aren't so obvious. Patches of green snake through the fault-lines. Today I close my eyes as I walk. Pointing at random when I open them.

That's my new spot.

But it's not. So I go back.

If he knew my tree fell, there'd be no *I told you so*. He'd just tell me to be more careful. He'd tell me about something I already saw on the news. A few months ago a woman was killed by a falling tree while jogging her dog.

'You can be crushed without even trying,' is what he'd say. 'So imagine the odds when you're putting in a daily effort.'

Should I think of myself as a survivor? He'd say this: 'Statistics are statistics.

You never feel like it'll happen to you until it does.'

He told me never to swim at the top of waterfalls and never to drive through floodwaters. To always use the right charger and always point knives down in the dishwasher.

If only he gave more bad advice. The kind I'd feel better about forgetting.

By the end of the week the new grass is blended in. You'd only see cracks if you knew where to look. All that's left is a crevice in the path where roots went through it.

For the first time since the storm I eat lunch at lunch. Legs parallel with the invisible turf-scars, absorbing the worst UV of the day.

He said you shouldn't spend more than twenty minutes in the ten-'til-two sun. My break is thirty, but I'm trying to keep things in perspective.

My spot must be safer than before.

So I press my back against the ghost-trunk. Count the ducks. Keep chewing my pasta where the shade should be.

A New Sun

Hannah Goldstein

The sun was neon pink—luminescent, chemical, harsh—and absurdly round. The sky had burnt away entirely. All that remained was bone-grey space. It was going on five in the evening, but you wouldn't know it; this new sun was timeless, like plastic. Lena was captivated by the strangeness of it all, but given that nobody else had stopped dead in the street, she reasoned that she had probably misread the situation—read catastrophe where there was none. After all, the fires were elsewhere. Her attention was dragged back to ground level by the pulling of the leash. The greyhound, Ruby, having grown bored with the neighbour's recycling bin, now pressed onwards.

Lena took a deep breath, trying hard to relax as they crossed the road. The air was thick with smoke and petrol fumes. The asphalt shimmered in the heat. Lena gripped the leash. Cars had a habit of charging down here and she didn't entirely trust herself with the dog. She was not what you would call a dog person. She was fond of Ruby, which was why she had agreed to babysit Kathy's beloved canine for a few hours, but that casual, easy friendliness that dog-people possessed was foreign to her. Lena had no pets of her own.

Once they reached the park, she tried to relax into the role of a woman walking her dog. She smiled at the other dog walkers as though she were one of them. *Everything is fine*, she thought, *everything is good*. The churning in her stomach didn't make any sense at all. Only a few weeks earlier, she had moved into one of those new apartments in Marrickville with her boyfriend who packed her lunch every day. Each morning, when she looked around at the new white walls and smelt fresh coffee, she thought, *jesus*, and felt a little shy around her own life, careful not to touch anything lest it should break.

Ruby stopped and eyed a small yappy dog that was playing with some children up ahead. Kathy had warned her that Ruby did not like small dogs and Lena braced herself for trouble. She imagined the small ginger fluffball in

Ruby's powerful jaws—the crunching of small bones, tearing of flesh. Would she leap to the rescue? Run away? Stand in silent horror and watch it? But Ruby trotted calmly by. A wave of pride surged through Lena.

'You're a good dog, aren't you?' she crooned. 'You're a good dog.' It felt like the most genuine thing she had said in a while.

Perhaps it was the smoke that was making her stomach churn. A greasy, brown haze had fallen over Sydney in the past few days as fires tore their way across the country. On the news, the anchor had looked down the barrel of the camera and announced that the air quality was at dangerous levels. People with asthma were advised to stay indoors. Lena suddenly felt a little frightened to be outside in the park. She regretted the deep breaths that she had taken and worried that she had done permanent damage to her lungs. She glanced up at the evil-looking sun—syrupy, poisonous pink. She imagined herself and Ruby in gas masks, fighting their way through black smoke; the last two creatures on earth. Perhaps this was how things would always be now. But then a jogger in a Lululemon sports crop-top and tights smiled as she passed by and Lena felt better.

Only that morning, Lena had been offered a new job. A great job. She would be closer to home and in a brand-new building. A bit more money too. Her boyfriend had hugged her. Her parents had called to congratulate her. On the radio, Lena had heard that fire had driven people to the beaches. That there had been nowhere to go but the sea.

Lena and Ruby did laps around the oval. Round and round. She would have to get new clothes for work. The thought made her feel strangely tired.

'You're a good dog, aren't you?' It was comforting, to talk to someone without any expectation of conversation. No meaning to be shared or lost. Round and round. There was no grass left on the oval. Some kids kicked a soccer ball through the dust.

As they approached the tennis courts, they were suddenly accosted by a man with dyed blonde hair and his muscular dog.

'Sorry, didn't mean to scare you,' the man said, embarrassed at having taken her by surprise. 'Thought you were Kathy … we've been socialising Prince and Ruby.'

His dog, Prince, danced around Ruby as she stared on, unimpressed.

'Oh right,' said Lena, smiling wide in an effort to mask the fact that she'd gasped at his approach.

'Where's Kath?' he asked.

'Her mum's 70th tonight. We're neighbours and I'm her only friend without plans on a Friday night.'

He laughed. 'Makes two of us.'

Ruby lurched forward and Lena tightened her grip on the leash.

'We can let them have a run around on the tennis courts if you like?'

'You mean off the leash?'

'Yeah, give 'em a chance to mess around. What do you think?'

Lena hesitated. 'Sure.'

'Cool.'

The four of them headed towards the tennis court. Lena felt Ruby become more and more excited as they approached. She hoped that she would be able to get the leash back on when it was time to go. Nightmarish visions of herself chasing an errant greyhound through all the streets of Marrickville coursed through her mind.

They stepped through the gate. Lena unclipped the leash. Ruby immediately headed for the net. Prince chased her. Ruby darted around it and Prince, momentarily confused, circled the umpire's chair, then, seeing Ruby down the other end of the court, gave chase.

'I'm Lena by the way.'

'Ari.'

'Super weird day, huh?' said Lena, cringing at the glossy vocab she'd apparently picked up from somewhere.

Ari shrugged. 'It's just the fires, I guess. They're burning all over the place.'

'Yeah, it's terrible isn't it?'

Lena found that she had an urgent desire to talk about the fires but Ari wasn't interested.

They watched the dogs. Their play became rough. They chased each other faster and faster, their large paws slapping the ground. They leapt and barked. Lena pictured teeth and blood but when she looked to Ari he just watched them calmly so she thought that perhaps she was overreacting. She hoped that he didn't see that she was afraid, but when the dogs came hurtling passed her, she flinched, not knowing how you could tell the difference between play and violence.

'They're alright,' said Ari reassuringly, as he bent down and patted Prince.

'Yeah, they're so cute,' and again she cringed at her own voice.

Lena bent down next to Ari and patted Prince to prove that she was unafraid. Ruby lay down by the net and yawned. Lena felt the heat radiate from Ari's skin. She suspected that the UV rating was high even though it was going on five thirty and she tried to calculate how long it had been since she'd last applied sunscreen.

'So you live nearby?' Ari brushed Lena's shoulder as he shifted his weight and drew Prince closer in.

'Just down the street.' Sweat ran down her leg. *God, she must stink*, she thought. Ari was sweating too; he glistened brown.

'We could hang out sometimes … you know, on Friday nights when we have nothing better to do.'

Lena laughed. She thought of her boyfriend, their apartment with the new white walls.

'Yeah,' she said. 'Sure.'

She typed Ari's number into her phone without much thought. It alarmed her, sometimes, the lack of interest she felt in her own life.

Lena and Ruby walked home. The sun beat down on them. Lena's skin felt itchy and tight. She thought of the cicada shells she had collected as a kid, dried out bodies, husks left behind. Perhaps those summers spent camping and swimming were gone. Now summer meant fire and smoke.

Ruby panted heavily. 'Almost there, girl, almost there.' Lena pictured herself in her nice clean bathroom, stepping into a cool shower, washing it all away. She suddenly wondered what would happen if she turned down the job. Called back and said she'd had a change of heart. She could do it. The HR woman's number would be in her call list. What would she do then? Have an affair with Ari? Then beg for forgiveness? Fight until the neighbours complained? Maybe even throw a plate and leave a mark on the wall. She could ruin everything—so easily, so shockingly easily. And the strange sun seemed to call her to it.

Somehow it all seemed so sad, so unbearably sad—not the thought of ruining everything but the thought that things should go on like this, that she should go on like this.

'What should I do?' she asked Ruby. The dog actually looked up at her with those dark placid eyes.

It took Lena a moment to realise that she was standing outside Kathy's flat. There was her friend, dressed in a plum party dress, sprawled out on the dried-up lawn, holding her phone to the sky.

'Look Lena! Look at the sun!' Lena lay down next to Kathy. Kathy looked for the best filter. Ruby stuck her snout in Kathy's handbag. Lena closed her eyes. She was so tired.

'It looks like the end of the world, eh Lena? It's kind of beautiful.'

'You think so?'

'In an apocalyptic kind of way.'

Lena took a deep breath and smoky air filled her lungs. It was a relief to finally talk about it, to know that Kathy too recognised an ending of some kind.

They lay there until the sun dipped below the newest and biggest of the apartment complexes. Laying there, on the solid earth in the near-dark, Lena felt herself back away from catastrophe. Of course she would take the job. Of course she would go home to her boyfriend. There was nothing to worry about but the usual things which weren't even really worth worrying about anyway. She would go back to her apartment. He would gather her in and put on the air con. Probably even make dinner—he was a good cook. And the old sun would come back, soon enough. They might even get a dog.

Divergence

Nicole Hodgson

I stood on the hillside like a sentinel. Watched. Waited. Pleaded with the storm clouds to come closer. If only I were a rainmaker. A shaman, some kind of witch. I would shake a rattle at the sky, mutter some incantations. I would do anything to bring about change.

But the sky resisted my pleas. Hulking bulkheads of cloud, the stern grey of a battleship and so enormous they cast a shadow on the unsettled Southern Ocean. A swathe of rain fell out onto the water and blurred the line between sky and sea. The cold front had slipped to the south again. All that rain, where it is not needed, or so desperately wanted.

We had been warned, of course. The signs were there. But nobody imagined it could all change so quickly.

On the back of the laundry door an ancient clipboard hung on an old rusty nail. For over a hundred years a member of the Horton family has methodically recorded rainfall and temperature every single day on neatly lined sheets. Completed sheets are bundled into archive boxes then piled up in the sleep-out. I put a large O in the rainfall column for the 21st of June. And could have wept at the long line of zeros.

I took a cup of tea to the shed where Will was bent over the workbench, intent, focused. I called out over the blaring radio, but he didn't hear.

'Jesus!' he said, when I appeared next to him. 'You scared me!'

But he grabbed me for a moment, affectionate bear of a man that he is, and I was momentarily smothered by his flannel shirt that smelled faintly of dirt and grease, but mostly the familiar comfort of him.

'What are you up to?' I asked when he let me go.

'Messing around with the planter.'

I stopped myself from saying, *but we can't plant anything more until it rains.* He didn't need reminding.

'Have you been over to the new patch today?'

Last winter's seedlings, in desperate need of a drink.

'Yeah,' he said, without looking at me. 'They're hanging in there. Just.'

A bit like us.

'We won't be getting any rain out of this. I watched it all fall out on the ocean.'

'Yep. Figured as much.'

Not true. He'd been saying for days that this strong front would be the drought-breaker.

'Will ... we've got to make some decisions.'

He stopped. Slapped his hands down on the bench.

'Don't push me, Elsa. Don't bloody push me.'

I could so easily have pushed. Desperate for a reaction, some movement, his solid tenacity was suddenly infuriating. But I heeded his warning, for now, and turned away.

I whistled for Tess who panted at my heels. Close to the farmhouse we walked over crisp grass dried to a palette of beige and brown. When I first came here, black cattle ranged these hills covered, then, in bright green pasture even in the middle of summer. 1000mm of rain will do that. The cattle are long gone and we are farming carbon now. I often wonder what Will's great-grandfather would make of us, trying to plant back all the trees.

Gritty optimism must be genetic. How else could an English soldier, not long back from the trenches and faced with a hillside of towering karri forest be anything but overwhelmed. He was given a tent, a few supplies and an axe and told he could keep this patch of land only if he cleared at least half of the trees. Now, the only way we can keep the farm is if we plant them all back.

I crouched down beside last year's seedlings, the dirt so dry it fell off my fingers like powder. All the leaves curled, some turning brown. The seedlings are not hanging in there. They are dying.

That's more like us.

Tess and I kept walking, towards the back boundary, up and down the rolling hills that used to look like some Anglophile's dream. Now they are striped by the discomforting lines of a struggling tree plantation, where even the older saplings were showing signs of stress. Dead trees don't absorb any carbon. Dead trees are like a set of matches, stuck into the ground, ready to ignite. People in town are always muttering about whether this summer will bring the big fire that's got to be heading our way. Or else they are on their knees in the small weatherboard churches, praying for rain.

They ought to be praying for the drowning Bangladeshis, the Indians dying of thirst, for all the people fleeing the Middle East. Where things are truly catastrophic, instead of just really bad. Personally, I've given up on thoughts and bloody prayers. If there is a God she's got her headphones on and the music blaring, just like our kids on the rare occasion they make the trek down from the city. I've taken that up with our eldest, but all she'll say is that it is too depressing to come back.

The dog and I walked to the back of the farm, to the patch that was never cleared, a remnant of the original forest that once covered this whole place. Walking in there is to cross a threshold, into a darker, quieter world. Amongst the towering straight-trunked karris are patches of soft sheoaks. They leave a carpet of needles behind that softens and muffles everything. Curling green vines twine over the undergrowth. In here it is green and moist in a way that the rest of the farm has forgotten how to be. As though here amongst the oldest, wisest beings there is knowledge about how to adapt, how to flex to changing circumstances, a wisdom inaccessible to youngsters and newcomers. Not Will and me. In our early sixties we just seem to be getting more rigid. Age has only calcified us.

That night the bed felt enormous. A dead zone down the middle that we did not broach, smothered in an oppressive silence. Finally I couldn't handle it anymore. I reached out to touch Will's hip, his thigh. He rolled away to the edge of the bed, the brief affection of the afternoon forgotten.

We've been together so long that our libidos are like shy marsupials that will only occasionally creep out from the forest. Jumpy. Easily spooked. To get both creatures out into the clearing at the same time without frightening one or both back into the undergrowth—that's a rarity now. But Will was doing more than just refuse my tentative advances.

I sat up in bed and turned on the lamp.

'Come on. Talk to me.'

He stayed on his side. Grunted.

'You can't ignore me forever.'

He sighed and turned over onto his back. In the old days, he would curl towards me, cradle his head in his hand. Now he lays with his arms by his side, on top of the doona, like he's in a hospital bed.

'What?'

'You know what. We can't afford to do this anymore. Last year's seedlings are dead. We'd need to truck water to keep the others alive. We're broke, Will.'

'I've been talking to the bank.'

I closed my eyes for a moment to still the rage.

'Don't be ridiculous. We can't handle any more debt.'

'You could work more.'

'You bastard. That is so unfair. You know how hard I've been trying to get more work. More dead-end work that I'm totally over-qualified for. There are no jobs. The town is dying.'

'We just need one good season.'

He is deluded.

'But you know there won't be any more good seasons. It's over, Will. I can't spend another summer here, freaking out about fire.'

He shook his head. His mouth set hard.

'We've got to stick it out. I'm not fit for anything else. Or anywhere else.'

'We can't stick it out. We have to go to the city—that's the only place there's any work.'

'And do what? You might be alright but what the hell would I do with myself?'

'I don't know—you could get work as a mechanic? You could retrain and work at the food farms?'

He scoffed.

'Retrain? Whose gonna bother with an old bugger like me? Besides I wouldn't go near those weird food factory places.'

'We have to do something, Will.'

He doesn't have the words but, if he could, I think he'd tell me that if this place is in my heart, then it is lodged in his very marrow. He is as rooted here as one of his trees. Invisible mycorrhizal threads link him to this patch of earth in a mysterious symbiotic relationship that I don't fully understand. I mourn the loss of that, for him, but it is not enough anymore. Not for me.

'I can't leave, Elsa. I'll never leave.'

'And I can't stay.'

And there it was.

The convergence that we've been approaching as steadily as an artist sketching a perspective line. Two lines actually, in a sketch of a road or a path that start far apart, but eventually join in a single point on the horizon.

Only this junction of ours is one of divergence and wrenching separation.

The Smell Of A Dog

Greg Burgess

Emma and David weren't like other parents, it was as if they had never got used to being a family. They even wanted Robert to call them by their first names—though he never did—and were forever inviting people over, as if they were afraid of being on their own, just the three of them.

When there were visitors Robert stayed up until the last one had left, no matter how late. He would sit on the floor in a corner of the room, reading a book or playing electronic games. Some nights he just watched the adults.

If anyone asked why he wasn't in bed, his parents looked puzzled, as if the idea hadn't occurred to them. It's up to him, they said.

One woman, who had a seven-year-old as well, couldn't bear to see Robert on his own. She sat cross-legged beside him and asked the usual things: Did he like school? What would he be when he grew up?

Robert stared at her. He didn't want to grow up, not if you had to sit around all night laughing at nothing. But it was no good telling her that.

The noise at the dining table died down. The others knew it was best to leave Robert alone, but the woman hadn't met him before.

'A footballer? A fireman?' she persevered.

Robert still didn't answer.

'A politician,' someone called out.

'He's great with tech stuff,' said Emma.

That was true. Robert was top of his IT class and could fix his parents' phones whenever they messed them up. But stuff like that was only for filling in time. He liked real things, things you could touch, things with a smell: the mud on the school oval in winter; freshly cut wood in his grandfather's workshop. He liked the smell of a dog.

Robert's birthday arrived.

He woke early, as always, and lay in bed staring up into the darkness. For Christmas, his grandparents had given him a planetarium of luminous stars, comets, and supernovas to help pass the night, but the miniature universe had never been glued to the bedroom ceiling. It had stayed in the box untouched, but not because his parents cared about the look of the room or any marks the adhesive might leave—David and Emma weren't like that. Their place had the feel of a share house, like the one where they'd first met—there were cheap prints on the walls, old wooden chairs that didn't match the steel and glass dining table, and vases always empty of flowers.

When it was light, Robert put on his school clothes and went into the living room. David, still in pyjamas, was slouched on the sofa. He looked up from his phone.

'Hey, little man. How do you like Cyril?'

'Who's Cyril?'

David nodded towards the kitchen. The benches were covered with glasses and pots and plates from the dinner party the night before, but, in a small, cleared space sat a plastic fish tank. Its base was the size of a sheet of paper, but the sides sloped outwards, making it a little bigger at the top. Darting from one end to the other, either exploring its new home, or else trying to find a way out, was a gold and orange fish, about as long as Robert's middle finger.

A card with a large number 8 on the front was propped up against the tank. Robert glanced at the few words scrawled inside, then put it back down.

'I wanted a dog.'

David pulled himself up off the sofa and came over to make his breakfast, roughing up Robert's hair as he passed. Robert smoothed it back down.

'A fish is a great pet. I wish I'd had one when I was a kid.'

Cyril swam into a tiny plastic grotto in one corner of the tank. After a few seconds he came out again.

'His tank is too small.'

Emma appeared at the door, already in her work clothes.

'Does he like it?'

The fish swam a circuit of the tank, stopping near Robert's face.

'I wanted a dog.'

On Sundays, Robert's parents never emerged from their bedroom until it was time to go out for brunch.

Robert hated the cafe. It was crowded and noisy, and they sat at a big table where he got squashed between David and Emma, or even between one of them and a stranger. He would nibble at a muffin while his parents ate huge meals and talked, even to people they'd never met before. And if there were other children, they wanted him to go and play with them, as if it was as easy as that.

The part of the morning before going to the cafe was almost as bad; it was like being at the dentist before you went in. All he could do was stare out the window and wait.

But now there was Cyril.

The fish hadn't made Robert any happier. Watching Cyril swim round and round the tank upset him, in the way that some people are upset by the sight of animals in pens at the zoo.

He told Martin about it, one lunch time. They were sitting under a tree at the edge of the school oval.

Martin wasn't interested. His place had a dog and cat and a couple of chooks; he couldn't see the point of a fish.

'Goldfish only remember the last three seconds,' he said. 'It can't get bored.'

Robert had heard that as well, but it wasn't true. When he approached the tank, container of food in hand, Cyril swam straight to the surface, waiting for the flakes to fall—he knew. But Martin was like an adult, he wouldn't listen if Robert tried to explain.

'What about the dog?' asked Martin.

Robert had never stopped asking for one, but David and Emma hadn't given in. They'd gone on about smells and soiled rugs, annoyed neighbours, and Body Corporate rules, but the truth was, they couldn't be bothered with a dog, that was all.

'Bastards,' said Martin.

Robert bit his lip and frowned; he'd never thought of his parents like that. They were stupid and annoying sometimes, but it wasn't their fault, it was just the way they were.

A ball rolled towards them, a small boy chasing after it. Martin stopped the ball with his foot, then kicked it further away.

'Promise you'll do something good if they give you a dog,' he said. 'Or stop doing something they don't like.'

Robert shook his head. David and Emma didn't much care what he did.

'Have they got any secrets?'

Robert didn't know any.

'Look on their phones.'

David was at a staff meeting.

Someone was droning on about budgets and performance targets, and the room was too hot, but he didn't care. He was thinking about Natalie.

She had this cute way, when she caught sight of him, of giving a sly smile and a little half-wave, as if she was afraid of someone noticing.

The man at the front of the room put up another slide.

She'd be at the gym when he got there, and later … he stretched his legs and arched his back in anticipation.

Raised voices interrupted David's daydream: an argument had broken out over office reallocations. He listened for a while, then took out his phone. There was no need to hide it—half the people in the room had their head down, looking at some device or other, multi-tasking.

He opened his emails—one with the subject '*Puppy*' had just come in. He clicked on it.

Dear Daddy
please can I have a puppy soon
Your son Robert

David groaned. He was fed up with the dog business.

Part of a photo was visible below Robert's words, and David scrolled down to see what it was.

His finger froze. On the screen was a picture he'd taken one night at Natalie's place. Their faces were squashed together, not exactly kissing, but you could tell they were more than friends. Underneath the image was pasted the sign off from Natalie's text messages:

Love ya Davey
N xxx

Emma and her friends were at their usual table—the one out the front, where they could be as loud as they liked—and the barista had just brought out their coffees.

On the edge of Emma's saucer was a small teddy-shaped biscuit.

'How are my special ladies today?'

They bantered with Vijay about his gym-sculpted muscles until he was called back to the counter.

'Nice bum,' said Jenny.

Ping.

They all checked their phones.

'It's from Robert,' said Emma. 'He's a funny kid—he sends these really serious messages, like he's writing to a stranger.'

Everyone laughed.

'Dear Mummy,' she read out loud, 'please can I have a puppy …'

Emma rolled her eyes. 'Not that again,' she said, swiping her finger up the screen. A photograph appeared.

'Isn't that Vijay?' said the woman sitting next to her.

Emma snapped the phone cover shut.

'He's a weird little kid.'

Robert's parents both left work early the next day—David wrote an email saying he wasn't feeling well, and Emma told her boss she had a client to visit —but they didn't get home until late afternoon. They arrived at the apartment block entrance at the same time, but from different directions, and David slowed to let Emma drive in first.

After they had parked, each of them took from their car a cardboard pet carrier.

'What's that?' asked Emma.

'A puppy.'

'You said he couldn't have one.'

'What have you got?'

'A puppy. Take yours back—he can't have two.'

'I can't—I promised.'

'So did I.'

Emma and David's eyes met for a few seconds, then they both looked away. Emma was about to say something when a whimpering sound came from one of the boxes.

It's getting cold,' said David, 'we'd better go in.'

The puppies were running around the apartment, slipping and sliding on the polished floor—and Robert was laughing.

Emma squeezed David's hand. They'd got him the fish and now the two dogs—they were good parents, really. She was leaning against David's shoulder and he was running his fingers through her hair.

After a time, the dogs tired themselves out and curled up in a corner to sleep. Robert went to the kitchen bench; it was time for Cyril's evening meal. He shook out some flakes and the fish swam up, plucking them off the top of the water. When the last flake was gone, Robert said he was taking the puppies into his room. Emma smiled and said that was alright.

David and Emma went to their bedroom as well.

Half an hour later, both their phones pinged. David leaned across to the bedside table. Robert had sent the message.

Tomorrow, you are going to buy Cyril a bigger tank.

Whitecaps

Sean Wilson

'I want to see the ocean,' he says.

He says it in a casual tone, as if he's asking her to pass the salt. A simple request. But when she turns and looks at him, lying there, as thin as she's ever seen a person, a sheet where there should be blankets, she sees a pleading in his eyes. This is not something she can turn down. This is not something she can refuse.

She grinds her teeth at every bump on the highway. She strangles the steering wheel with both hands. The shock absorbers on her old Mitsubishi feel like hardwood carved into the car. He's in the passenger seat, tensing and relaxing. Tensing and relaxing. Potholes in the shoulder of the road and tree roots snaking under the bitumen. Every shift in the highway surface rattles his body. He wears clothes that look like hand-me-downs. They look like an older brother or cousin's clothes, passed to him too early. She knows this isn't the case. He bought the grey hoodie and black tracksuit pants he's wearing. They belong to him. These are comfortable clothes, bought long before everything changed. They're all wrong for the season. There's far too much material for the weather. He needs the extra layers these days. Without the layers, his teeth rattle and his hands shake.

'Which beach?' she asks. She's making her voice bright, pulling it up to a higher pitch. 'Do you have a preference? We could get some chips or something.'

'I'm not sure,' he says. 'I don't want to ruin my appetite for the meal tonight. They're serving something brown with something green in the ward. It might even have some texture.'

She laughs, a few short bursts. Forcing it out, performing for him. She wants to calm him, to soothe him. She doesn't feel amused. The thought of him picking up a spoon and pushing around meal after meal of measured calories makes her want to drive all day, to keep driving and driving until the petrol tank is dry. She wants to reach for the horizon, to push out past the barrier, to speed over to the other side of whatever this is.

She parks in the first row of spaces in the beach car park, under the shade of a wide gum tree and facing the deep, blue Indian Ocean. There's a breeze out on the water, out there on the other side of the windshield, whipping up whitecaps that shift and move in her vision. The sun is dipping low in the sky, down toward the ocean, hidden now behind a streak of pale clouds. She opens the door and a smell rushes to her. It smells of spring flowers, pollen and salt.

'Can we sit here for a minute?'

He shifts his body in the seat, eyes fixed on the movement out on the water. She watches his face. She sees it soften, sees the lines around his eyes smooth out as he takes a deep breath. She sees the skin around his cheekbones, so tight it looks set to tear, rest a little. The grey hairs at his temples, the first sign of the end of his twenties, shine in the afternoon light.

She remembers the night they met. It was four years ago. A storm had settled over the city, one of those storms pulled in by the thick cold fronts that roll over the coast year after year. The rain was coming in at an angle, getting under the hood of her raincoat, messing up the hair she'd teased into submission. She was in a hurry. She was fifteen minutes late. She turned toward the door of the bar and shook the wet coat from her body.

It was what her parents might have called a blind date. They'd been chatting for two weeks on the app that brought them together. He'd been witty and attentive where others had seemed needy and desperate. He'd given it time but not so much time that the moment could pass. She remembers feeling excited for the first time in months as she made her way through the crowd in the bar. She remembers hoping that this one would be different. That he would be different.

He was sitting at the bar, holding a drink to his lips, eyes scanning the room. When he saw her, his face softened, his eyes almost closing as he watched her. They said hello, moving together for a quick hug, the rain passing from her cheek to his.

'What are you drinking?' she asked.

'A gin and tonic,' he said. 'I would've ordered you one but I didn't want you to have to send it back. You know, with people drugging drinks and all.'

She remembers scanning his face then, passing it over, looking for signs that should cause her alarm. It was the first time she looked at him that way, the first time she took in his features. There was nothing bad in his face.

'There's so much to think about on dates. I don't know if I would've thought of that,' she said. 'Anything else I should be aware of?'

'Only the prices in here,' he said. 'They'll send us broke. We might have to water down the next round.' He ordered her a drink and she reached into her bag, moving her phone around between her thumb and index finger. She couldn't have known which way the date would go but she remembers feeling, at that moment, like she wanted to delete the app from her phone.

'I think I'm ready to walk now,' he says.

She helps him out of the car and they walk until they reach a bench. There's a footpath in front of them that winds above the edge of the sand and, down below, the groups of bronzed people lying on towels and hitting volleyballs back and forth. There's the low sound of waves breaking against the shore and, above that, the higher sounds of beachgoers squealing and shouting. His skin is paler than the sand. He breathes like he's run a mile.

'Say the word and we'll go,' she says.

'No, no,' he says. 'I'm enjoying myself. I'd like to stay out here a while.'

Two seagulls glide down from the trees and land near their bench. They turn their heads side-on, staring with flat eyes. One of the seagulls stands on a single leg. She can't tell if the other leg is missing or if it's pulled up close to the body. She feels primed to search for destruction and disease, her eyes scanning for a diagnosis.

'That's right,' she says. 'I was going to get us some chips. You fine if I go get some?'

'Of course,' he says, nodding under the hood of his jumper. 'I'll just do some exercise to pass the time. You know, work on my muscles in the sun.'

She walks quickly to the cafe, cutting through the grass. She knows that she's been moving faster than usual. She feels as though she's trying to outrun something. She's felt herself wanting to break into a run at work, at home, at the supermarket. She's felt a need to move, further and further, faster and faster. She's been trying to put some distance between herself and something but she's not sure what, and she's not sure what direction she would need to point her body to get away from it.

When she comes back with the bag of chips, oil seeping through the paper and onto her hands, she sees him slumped to one side on the bench. Her breath catches and she stops walking. She watches him, counting instinctively in her mind. One, two, three, four, five. One, two, three, four. He moves. His arm moves around his body and he reaches for his back, rubbing at a muscle that's hard to find. She sighs and continues walking.

'I got vinegar,' she says. 'I hope that's alright.'

He pulls his arm away and shifts his body on the bench. He lifts his chin at the package, sniffing the air.

'Seems appropriate,' he says.

She lays the chips down on the bench between them and they take turns dipping into the bag. They chew slowly, watching waves curl away from the groyne. They watch surfers rise on their boards and drop back down to the water. They see a man pacing along the beach, waving a metal detector in front of his feet. They see women wearing bikinis, rubbing sunscreen on their shoulders.

'Do you think you'll find someone else?'

She looks at him. He's facing the ocean. She watches his jaw move as he eats, the skin tight around his face.

'What do you mean?'

'You know,' he says. 'After, of course. Not before. I wouldn't like that.'

He turns and winks at her. He smiles but she can see the corners of his mouth shake a little.

'Don't talk about it,' she says. 'Please. Not here. Not now.'

'Okay,' he says.

Two small children wearing bathers and thongs, floaties strapped to their arms, run past the bench. They turn on the path and run away, toward the surf lifesaving building. Their father runs behind them, calling out for them to stop, one hand pressed to the bridge of his nose, holding his glasses in place.

'It's funny,' he says, holding a chip up in front of his face and studying it. 'The body exaggerates the size of everything. Do you know what I mean? This chip, this chip right here, it's so small compared to me. It's tiny compared to my body but as soon as I put it in my mouth, it'll feel huge. It'll feel immense. It'll feel like everything. All my attention will be on this chip and it'll feel so big, moving around inside my mouth, getting carved up by my teeth. They'll feel huge too, my teeth. It'll feel like that's all that matters, what's going on inside my mouth. This single chip and my teeth, they'll be so, you know, significant to me.'

He puts the chip in his mouth and starts to chew. There's a silence that falls between them. The only sound comes from the waves and the distant screams and the wind passing through the leaves above them. She stares at the ocean, blue and white shifting, rising and falling. One colour appearing then the other colour replacing it, never staying one way for long.

'It's like the tumour in my body,' he says, staring out at the ocean. 'It's so small compared to the rest of me. It's tiny when you think about it and that's just my body. Compared to the world and the sun and all the other planets and stars in the universe, it's insignificant. It's nothing, really. But it's the one thing that matters right now. To me, it's everything.'

She watches him take the last chip from the bag and place it in his mouth. He picks up the bag and then folds it, end over end, until it's almost the size of a postage stamp. He pushes the folded bag down into a gap between the wood of the bench. She looks at him, at his wet eyes, white next to blue. They were only starting out. They were at the beginning of everything and now this. She sees him shiver under his clothes.

'Do you think we should go now?'

'Not yet,' he says, eyes fixed on the whitecaps out there on the ocean. 'Please. I want to stay a little longer. Just a bit longer.'

Tattoos

Ben Brooker

1. Rain

Nim wanted to walk home in the rain. Bess didn't. He said it would be romantic. She said it wouldn't; they would just catch colds. He said he liked the way her hair looked after rain—untamed, anarchic. She said walking home in the rain was what they did in Woody Allen movies, and that she could not bear to think of Woody Allen movies anymore. He said neither could he, but that it happened in Richard Curtis movies too. She could not bear, she told him, to think of Richard Curtis movies either, and that that had nothing to do with who Richard Curtis was as a person—it was just that, in her opinion, all of them except *Four Weddings and a Funeral* were unwatchable. Nim agreed, and hailed a cab. He sat up front, because he did not want to be the kind of person who did not, and she squeezed in behind the driver's seat. The cab, they both thought, smelt new, vaguely chemically, as though its upholstery had recently been laundered. She gazed at him, his face in profile, wondering what it was about his soft jaw, his fleshless nose, his uneven stubble and large ears that had first endeared him to her. He had made her laugh, Bess guessed, at a time in her life when she had not been disposed to do so. He looked back at her once, like Orpheus in the underworld, but by then she had turned away, a poster for a museum of anatomy catching her eye. On another day she might have suggested they go there, make the most of their day, not return to the hotel until late. But it was not another day. It was this day. And it was raining, like in a funny/sad movie she did not want to watch anymore.

She wanted pizza for dinner. There was a place, Bess said, that a friend had recommended, had eaten at every night of his three-month artist's residency. Nim wanted to go down to the hotel restaurant, the one on the mezzanine level that did cheap cocktails from four to six o'clock. They could have a cheap cocktail, she said, and then go for pizza. They did. He had a single white

Russian—hardly worth it in her opinion—she an espresso martini, which the bar staff had never heard of and had to Google. After that, something combining scotch and blood orange that she had seen in a TV show but could not afterwards remember the name of. The pizza was good, and reasonably priced. They agreed on the topping—margarita, no funny business, just fresh basil, a plainish sort of cheese, and a sauce, not too sweet, made with fresh tomatoes and a good quality olive oil. For dessert they had black coffee and almond biscotti. Afterwards, in the street, she had a cigarette. He did not. It had stopped raining. The night was warm and still, the sky a grim smudge above the big city. She watched him through the window as he paid the bill—'l'addition s'il vous plait,' she had seen him mouth at first, forgetting they were not in Paris anymore—and wondered how they would remember this night. There was that syndrome, she thought, that struck Japanese tourists when they arrived in Paris and found the city to be less than they had dreamed.

2. Brace

Bess had known her flight had been delayed since just after she had woken up in her hotel room at 5:00am. She had gone to the airport as planned anyway, arriving hours before her flight. She would not get back to sleep if she tried, and anyway the room had stopped making her happy. It had on the first night, with its luxurious sheets and hospital corners and faintly exotic view of the esplanade. But he had not showed up, and he had not answered her messages on the app. The room, once full of illicit promise, seemed to have grown cold in the increasing sureness that he was not coming, that, perhaps, he had been lying to her since the beginning. In the circumstances, she did not mind Ubering out into the cool 6:00am world, the hotel room—a coffin of silenced possibilities—receding into the bluish, pre-dawn distance behind her.

She had kept checking her phone in the Uber, nervous, panicky. What if something had happened to Nim? What if he had tried to get in touch but her phone wasn't working properly? Her phone was fine. He had texted. *Morning baby! Can't wait to see you. Safe travels! Xxx*. They had had a conversation about air safety before she had left for the conference she had told him she was going to, one of those hypnogogic late-night dialogues between couples that ebb and flow like a dream.

'The brace position kills more people than it saves,' he had ended up saying as she drifted near the brink of sleep. 'Breaks the neck.'

She thought this was bullshit, and told him so, only her language had been softer, more open. She had recalled hearing about a plane crash in which the only survivor had been the sole passenger to correctly assume the position. And hadn't there been an episode of *Mythbusters* about it? But she could not remember if the myth was that people who braced in air crashes died or did not die, and she could not remember what conclusion the hosts had reached. He had held her that night as he always held her—not spooning, but lying on his back with one arm outstretched, his palm resting on her hip or buttocks.

3. Ocean

It had worked for writers she knew about, Bess thought, as she looked out over the sea. Tennessee Williams had swum in it every day, the pills and alcohol seeping out of him. And Joseph Conrad had captained ships, hadn't he, forcing through the dark knot of his life? Troubled men, washed clean. But she thought of Virginia Woolf too, drowned, though not in the ocean, her overcoat full of stones.

A man was undressing near her, unembarrassed. She watched as he walked into the sea in his underwear, his long, thin legs rippling with the effort. She supposed he was about Nim's age. He even looked a little like him in his lean muscularity, his stubbly, almost lipless face and tousled brown hair. He had a small tattoo just below his right shoulder but she could not see what it was of. (Bess had a tattoo. Nim did not, though had talked about getting one with the frequency and intensity of someone who clearly has no intention of doing something.) The man had left on the beach his shorts and thongs, and an unzipped rucksack out of which was spilling a book, a can of deodorant, a set of keys, his wallet, a mobile phone, a Fitbit. Wasn't he worried about being robbed? Perhaps, she thought, he was not planning on coming back for them.

He did come back for them, fifteen minutes or so later, by which time she had received a text message from Nim. Going to read it, a temperature warning screen had flashed up: *iPhone needs to cool down before you can use it.* The phone, which had been lying exposed to the sun on top of her handbag, felt warm, but not hot. She wondered if it was overreacting, not that there was anything she could do about it except thrust it deeply into the cool dark of her bag and wait.

After checking his phone and laughing at something he had found on it, the man had unfurled his towel and shoved everything back into his rucksack. He then laid flat on his stomach, reading. She could still not make out the title, but its cover—oversized text, dark colours—suggested a cheap thriller.

Probably, she thought, he had quite sophisticated reading habits really but this was something he'd been saving for the summer holidays. A troubled man washed clean.

She tried her phone again. The screen, dark, would not be coaxed back to life. She had not heard from Nim in a month, and was worried. His mother had been sick—had something happened? Or was she fine, and he was getting in touch to say … what? That he wanted her to come back to him? Not by text, surely? She closed her bag, smeared some more sunscreen onto her face, and returned her attention to the man. He had turned onto his back now, was using his book to shield his face from the sun. His hair, suddenly, looked to be thinning on the crown, a portent of male-pattern baldness. The tattoo, now that he had moved, suspiciously resembled a Southern Cross. She thought of what Nim would say about the man, the tone of voice he would use. It had exhausted her, that tone, the studied viciousness of it. She had always wondered what it meant that he had never used it with her, only about other people when in her presence, not even when she did things she knew he secretly scorned like watching dating game shows or eating cereal when he wasn't around to make dinner. She thought of Woolf, of her overcoat full of stones. She tried to remember what she had written to Leonard in her suicide note, but could not.

4. Circle

In the beginning Bess had liked him to draw on her. Firm, but not hard enough to draw blood, or to leave a mark beneath the ink. She liked him to draw slowly—lines and waves, definite shapes. Circles especially. Closed and neat and whole. Always returning to their beginning, smoothly predictable. She thought he had a good hand. Steady. And he always asked—if he was pressing too hard, or had strayed too near somewhere sensitive. He never made her feel weird. When she asked him, just once, to see if she liked it, if he would press hard enough to make her bleed, he did. When she barked their safe word (she did not mean to bark, but that's what came out) he stopped. She liked that he liked it when she decided to leave one of his circles on her—a palm-sized ring just above her right hip—and have it made indelible by tattoo. She liked that he understood her frustration with friends and family who could not see the point of an empty circle. She liked that he got that her tattoo was too big to contain a name or an image. That it was too big to contain anything except possibility.

She thought, afterwards, about placing his name or likeness inside her circle but she could not, for he had made it clear there was no possibility of his coming back. Her lovers now trace it with post-coital fingers, and ask her what has faded from inside. He would never have asked such a question. Always, with these lovers, she returns to the same datum: *they are not you.*

Eid Ma Clack Shaw

Dan Prior

'What do you think it is?' asks Kelly, looking out the window at the abhorrent creature of poorly nailed offcuts and crocheted duct-tape that annexed half the back lawn. 'I mean, do you think he's actually building something or, you know, just building?'

'Hell if I know. He says he has no clue.' Sharon keeps her hand from her cheek by stirring the sugary sediment at the bottom of her cuppa.

'He needs to get his head to a shrink.' Kelly's eyes narrow as David walks from around the other side of the object, looking it up and down like a bogan Michelangelo before the marble. Oversized jumper, undersized footy shorts, thongs with the Aussie flag and a durry tucked behind his ear. 'Why doesn't he just tear it down?'

'He did,' says Sharon, blowing gently at her cuppa. 'Twice. He even had me tie him down to the bed one night, but he just screamed and thrashed around, speaking tongues like that woman in *The Exorcist*.'

Kelly laughs, 'Was his head spinning and spewing his guts up?'

'Nothing so much as that,' says Sharon, shaking her head. 'And he is seeing someone about it. We both are.' Sharon looks out the window at him. 'It really shakes him, you know. I mean, if it was sleepwalking, fair enough. That's something we could work out. But this?'

'It's like his work has become a nightmare.' Kelly says, stealing glances at Sharon's cheek.

'That's just it, he hasn't been doing any work. Sculptors just aren't in demand in this climate. It's been months since he last went into the workshop, even just for his own fun.'

She taps the spoon gently on the cup and seems to see through the table and into a space that is neither here nor now. And as she drifts into the memory, her hand unconsciously touches and rubs her cheek. Kelly turns and sees her chance to finally talk about the yellow and purple elephant in the room.

'When did that happen?'

'It's not what you think.'

'Oh, Shaz, it's always what I think. What happened? You tried to wake him up?'

Sharon moves her hand from cheek to cup. She sips and nods. 'I know the doctor said I shouldn't, but he was chanting. Like, I don't mean mumbling or talking in your sleep. He was chanting like he was praying to some cosmic being.'

Kelly looks at David pacing the object, scratching the back of his shaved head, kicking idly at weeds in the ground.

'So that's his excuse then?'

'It's not an excuse. It's what happened.'

Kelly's lips tighten. Eventually, another question slips through. 'What was he saying?'

'Just gobble-dee-gook. Weird shit, like, just sounds that he'd repeat over and over again. "Eid Ma Clack Shaw" or something like that. Reminded me of those prayers they do, you know, Muslims or Jews? Which ever one wears the funny hats and rock while they sing those paper rolls.'

'That's the Jews, I think.'

'Well, whatever, he was doing that and getting louder and louder. He'd stopped building, this was like, at 5am, just before the sun rose. I came out back and found him like that, rocking back and forth, *Eid Ma Clack Shaw! Eid ma Clack Sh—*'

'Shh,' Kelly says softly. They both look out the window. David turns from the house and back to the object. Like a kid with a guilty conscience, he moves to the back shed, searching for a purpose for his idling out of the house, other than avoiding their deliberation.

'So, when did he come round?'

'Not long after he hit me. I hit the floor and stayed there as he did that ... you know, that windmill thing that kids do when they fight? Flailing everywhere? Eventually he stopped and saw me. I was so angry I slapped him. But he didn't deserve it.'

'He did, Sharon, don't ever think otherwise.'

'No, I mean, he didn't mean to hit me. It was an accident.'

Kelly rolls her eyes. 'I suppose that's also some kind of accident?' Kelly gestures to the object.

'What do you mean?'

'Why do you think he's building it?'

'I don't know.'

'Come on, Shaz!'

'Come on what?'

'You said he started this back in, what, May?'

'Yeah.'

'And when did you find out about the pregnancy?'

Sharon breathes and looks at her friend, trying to remind herself that Kelly is only trying to be protective. 'No.'

'No what?'

'No to what you're thinking. That all this is some subconscious response of his to being a father. But it isn't. I didn't tell him straight away. I was too nervous. But then when he started his … new project, I had hoped the news might help him stop.'

'Men can know about these kinds of things. And David is a particularly sensitive soul.'

They both giggle at that. Sharon hopes that would be the end of it. But Kelly leans in.

'There is no—NO—excuse for his behaviour. Everyone knows he is eccentric, but this is something else. He's unbalanced.'

'The world is unbalanced, Kell. David's just out of work.'

'Don't use that as an excuse. He was already losing clients—and that was before everything happened. Most people are out of work and using that to behave how they want. What a convenient excuse to—'

'You think David is acting weird to get out of the relationship?'

Kelly bites her tongue and sits back in the chair. A clattering of wood comes from the shed, and David's faint cursing.

The women stare at each other, trying to make their points, trying to understand each other.

Kelly shakes her head. 'Of course I don't think that. He loves you. If he didn't, it'd be so much easier.'

'Easier to do what?'

'Shaz, come on. You're pregnant. Your partner's got a screw loose and has become dangerous. Are you really going to bring … ?'

She lets the rest hang in the air between them.

'You think I should leave him because he's a risk?'

Kelly shakes her head slightly, but, biting her lip, begins to justify. 'What if he did it to the baby? What if one night he puts it on the … the … —*that*, and starts chanting again. What if …'

Sharon puts her cuppa down with a clatter. She's heard enough.

'You think that I should leave him to protect myself and the baby. Kell, I love you, but—'

'Shaz, let me finish, you've got to start thinking of—'

'—no way, no way, am I going to leave him now, when he needs me the most. When I need him the most. When—'

'You're being foolish, he's not right, and it isn't safe here any—'

'—things might be tough but …'

'Damn it Shaz, listen to me will you? Listen!'

They stop, suddenly aware of the silence cowering before them. Sharon relaxes her jaw and Kelly unclenches her fist, laying it flat on the table, trying to smooth the tablecloth as easily as she would like to smooth things between them.

'I know you've both built a wonderful life together. Seriously, you make me and Geoff look like jealous teen lovers, bickering that we don't love each other as much as you do. But that doesn't mean you've got to put your safety at risk to stay with him.'

Sharon looks at her friend, collects their empty cups, and takes them to the kitchen. When she comes back out, Kelly is out of her chair, jacket on and slinging her bag over her shoulder.

'I'm sorry, Shaz.'

'Don't be.'

'No, I was a bitch just then.'

'It's alright, I know you're a bitch that cares.'

'I'm a bitch because I love you.'

They laugh and the friends embrace. They walk to the front door and speak softly to each other, making promises to catch up again next week. Kelly is a long time walking backwards, trying to make jokes as Sharon waits for her to turn so she can close the door. They wave and Sharon locks the front door after she sees Kelly's car pull away through the window.

She goes back into the kitchen with the intention of washing the cups, but never even touches the tap. She is startled when David appears behind her.

'Sorry love, you alright?'

'Oh, you gave me a jump.'

'You were just staring out the window. I was worried you might have caught my trances.'

'I don't think they're contagious.'

'Let's hope. How was Kell?'

'Kell was Kell. Full of good advice.'

'I'm sure. Did she leave instructions for how to knit a straight-jacket for me?'

'DIY lobotomy, actually.'

'Ouch.'

They laugh and he kisses her forehead and rubs her back.

'I was thinking, maybe I should try sleeping somewhere else. You know, go camping, get away from … my altar of madness.'

'Come on, babe, you don't need to do that.'

'Maybe I do. Maybe it's the safest thing …'

'I'm more worried you'll sleepwalk off a cliff than I am of you turning our backyard into a surreal landscape.'

He begins to argue and she puts her hands on his face.

'I don't care. I. Don't. Care. Whatever argument you've got rattling around in there. It's going to be just as bad as her advice. We will get through this, David. Baby, and sculpture of doom, both.'

David's shoulders relax. 'I might be mad, but you're the crazy one.'

'And don't you forget it.'

They kiss and he goes back out to the shed and she once again attempts to clean the cups.

As the tap runs and steamy water fills the sink, she falls back into her absent-minded stare. The object, abstract in design, maddening in its geometry. Maybe there's a reason for it. Some meaning, artistic or otherwise, that can be found in its twisting limbs and disturbing concept. Her hands fall to her belly.

The Game

Emma Rennison

'She's here!' I hissed through gritted teeth, my eyes wide. One side of my brother's mouth twitched and revealed a single dimple.

'Where? Where is she?' he said and ducked his head to my height, squinting past the pillar that divided the large open room.

'She's over there,' I whispered and directed him with a slight nod of my head. His smile became whole and his pupils darkened to black. He'd seen her.

The only things that got us through our parents' habitual Sunday afternoon pub visits were the range of cordials, the guarantee of a packet of prawn cocktail chips and the possibility of her presence. This weekend we scored a hat-trick. There she was, glowing like phosphorus across the smoky bar.

Translucent skin clung to her skull, exposing shadows that gave her concave cheekbones. Thick black liner charcoaled each eye, which emphasised their sunken dark holes, rather than any past beauty she may or may not have had. Jean Harlow brows framed them, tall and arched in permanent disapproval. Until she washed them off. Blood red lips matched the dress draped across her boney shoulders. Lavish and twinkling with sparkles as though she'd turned up at the wrong venue at the wrong time.

She dragged hard on a cigarette, a long gravity-defying trail of ash crept towards the filter. When she removed it her mouth remained in the exact same position as though the muscles didn't know what else to do. Small lines pinched around it from decades of this repetition.

Last of all, the part that fascinated us the most - the short black-blue curls of her hair, unnatural and wig-like, perched in perfect contrast against her pale ghastly skin.

We stared at each other, thrilled. The Ghost Lady was here.

I rested my chin on the dark wood bar as my dad ordered. Orange for me, lime for my brother. Our bartender, middle-aged and permed, poured fluorescent liquid into two tall glasses and blasted them with jets of water. With a trigger finger, she stopped and started the stream two or three times until full. A miniature wave sloshed over the side onto her hand as she pushed mine towards me.

We crab-walked through the round tables circled with mock leather chairs. Loudspeakers murmured the Top Forty and a synthesiser solo wove in and out of the conversational hum that filled the room. I shuffled past the back of a fat-necked man when he turned his head and blew cigar smoke into my face. I squeezed my eyes shut, but they stung and filled with water. I cleared my throat with my lips closed and hoped he wouldn't notice.

Smiles and backslaps greeted us when we found my parents' friends. Two tables pulled together were not enough room for everyone. My mum sat with the women. My dad stood to the side, with the men. They clasped their pots, glistening with dewy droplets, as they shuffled together. Voices loud and serious one moment, soft and normal the next.

My brother and I sat side by side. We were ready for the game.

'It's your turn,' he said. His eyes twinkled and I knew he had a plan.

'Oh no,' I moaned and dropped my chin to my chest.

'Oh yes,' he nodded, raising his brows in quick succession. 'You *have* to do it. You forfeited last time.'

'I didn't forfeit. I did what you told me to.'

'Nope. You were supposed to touch her hair and you chickened out,' he reminded me.

I glanced down in recollection. *How did he expect me to do that? I'd tried.*

'Today you have to walk past her and take a big deep breath and smell her.'

We stared at each other. I took a long sip of my drink. The cold orange rushed up the plastic straw and saturated my tongue.

'Easy,' I grinned. 'Watch.'

I stood, sidled between the two seats towards our victim. Each step slow, but not too slow, across the worn-down carpet filled with drunken bacteria.

I paused at the pillar dividing our table from hers and flattened my back and arms against it so she couldn't see me. I hadn't thought this through. I was too eager and hadn't checked my obstacles.

I twisted my body around the column and spied on her. She was with a friend. Just one. Perfect. As I let my breath out and shoulders relax she threw back her head and unhinged her jaw. Her raspy laugh filled my ears and every muscle in my body went rigid again.

Her companion stood, still smiling from their shared joke, and crisscrossed two empty wine glasses in one hand, her purse in the other. I needed a diversion. I needed to wait until the friend returned to distract her. It was too risky otherwise.

I reviewed my options, my mind clicking through them like the wheel of fortune. She was oblivious, her cigarette held between two gnarled and crooked fingers in a gesture I knew was rude. Her elbow balanced on the armrest as the smoke pirouetted above her head into nothingness.

I would check the roast of the day. And get napkins.

My brother stared at me, drinking, unblinking, enjoying the challenge.

I stepped out from my hiding place and scampered towards the specials board. Roast pork and apple sauce. My stomach rumbled. I fussed over a pile of napkins with nervous fingers.

'Can I help you?' the bartender said.

The napkins flew out of my hand to the floor. I pretended I didn't hear.

'Would you like to order?'

'No thanks. Just need these,' I said, avoiding eye contact.

She gestured for me to help myself. I scrunched up a handful and turned. My brother had his hands apart in a subtle question, his brows drawn together. I know, I know, I nodded back in reply.

She held her fresh wine up and clinked with her friend. I was close enough to see the powdery clogged creases embedded across her forehead and circling her mouth. Another line around the jaw separated her face and neck, soft and sagging and a more agreeable shade of pink.

Her lipstick imprinted the new wine glass. Her hollow eyes remained as black as the fake hair. If I looked at them for too long I feared being turned to stone.

I stepped closer and with her head frozen in position, her eyes flashed and locked onto me. I became a statue, mid-step. My gaze, caught in hers, unable to blink. She scanned me, my nose, my mouth, my hair, and back to my eyes. A line of freezing sweat ran between my shoulder blades. I tried to lift my foot, to move, to run, but I was anchored. She'd cast a spell on me. A Ghost Lady spell.

Her friend glanced from me, back to her, to me again, and sipped her wine.

Our staring contest continued, her eyes blank and lifeless. My heartbeat thumped in my ears, counting each second as they ticked by. I knew what I had to do. If I didn't, the next dare would be worse. I tipped my head back a fraction, contracted my nostrils and filled my lungs.

Her lips peeled back to reveal an oversized grin full of large nicotine-stained teeth set in receding gums. My eyes widened. I leaned back on my heels, desperate to put distance between us. My body jerked as the pokie behind me sang out. Cheers roared as gold coins clattered into the plastic tray and overflowed onto the floor. Her head pivoted towards the celebration and broke the moment.

My stone body was fluid again. I blinked, twenty times or more, and brought the wetness back. My arms swung like pendulums and I dodged a labyrinth of chairs, tables, and a heavy tide of adults to plunge into my chair, sinking low.

'What happened?' my brother asked. I knew he wanted details to feast on.

'Shhh. We need to hide,' I whispered but he was fixated on her, ignoring my warning.

'Did she say something to you?'

'No, nothing. Just stared at me with her beady black eyes. It was horrible,' I looked at my parents, deep in conversation. Their drinks still full.

'So, what was it? Mothballs? Dirt? Damp wood from the coffin she sleeps in?'

I frowned. I did smell her, but my mind was blank.

'I think she put a spell on me. I didn't smell anything. My nose might not work ever!' I grabbed the remains of my cordial. Orange. I picked up my brother's. Lime. I fell back into my seat, relieved. My senses still worked.

'They're on the move!' my brother said. I followed his gaze to see the friend shrug her into a brown and cream fur coat. She probably killed the animal herself.

'I need to go,' I said. My voice cracked.

I tapped mum, but she motioned not to interrupt.

'What do we do?' I asked my brother. My eyes flitted around for an escape route.

'Nothing. We haven't done anything wrong,' he said. 'You went to get napkins.'

'I sniffed her. Right when she was looking at me.' I shook my head at him, amazed at his nonchalance.

'Here she comes,' he said. I shrunk lower into my chair and sipped at my drink. Loud slurping noises strained through the bottom of the straw.

She linked her arm into her friend's and took a delicate step as if her bones would break at any moment. Her head wobbled on top of her long neck. My brother's eyes glistened.

I held my breath and waited for her to lean down and tell everyone what I'd done. But she kept walking, each skeletal step brought her closer to me and my brother. We studied the floor; he to control his giggles, me to nudge and 'shhh'.

They paused.

I receded into my shoulders and lifted my head in slow curiosity, straw dangling from my mouth. She rummaged through her tiny bejewelled bag. Perhaps she had poison or a matchstick-sized voodoo doll. Maybe she was conjuring a curse. I drew my knees to my chest, pointing my toes to the floor, and waited for her to do her worst.

Her thin fingers, pinched together like a shadow bird, gripped a tiny gold vial. A high-pitched squeal caught in the back of my throat. This was it. She tilted her chin to the ceiling and peered at me under smudged heavy lids. A fine mist settled against her stretched skin. Within a split second, the scent hit. Floral, sweet and mellow. She smelt of lavender.

Helen

Claire Riley

The oak chest arrived on a Tuesday. Paul brought it home on the trailer, encased in grey blankets and secured with a trucker's hitch. It was darker than Kate remembered, and larger—at least a foot wider than the space she had cleared for it in the guest room. Cherry oak, patterned ornately on its sides, it was as though the trailer had transported it from an earlier time instead of from Burke Street, Waitara, where Kate's mother had lived for eighty-three years. The lavender and moth ball smell of those delicate little bags Helen used to hang inside her closet emanated from it in sickly waves.

Kate watched Paul carry it inside, his breath shallow, blowing tight little puffs of air through thin lips as he heaved it indoors.

'Just leave it in the spare room,' she told him.

He placed it in the corner, squaring it gently.

'Do you want to look inside?' he asked. His eyes were sympathetic, searching. 'We could ask your brother over,' he added.

Kate walked from the room, the lavender scent compelling her outwards, towards air that didn't cloy and cling to her, tug at her memories like a child at her mother's skirt.

'Dinner's at seven,' she said.

It was important the phone call did not come in the dead of night. She would not be alerted to her mother's death while she lay inert, exposed. There was no sleep for weeks.

'It's that bloody chest,' she said to Paul when he tried gently to ask how she was coping.

Kate closed the door on the guest room only to learn that this somehow heightened the noise it made, wheezing behind thin walls, whistling a little on the exhale. The guest room became an exclusion zone, too volatile to approach.

It was a Thursday when the call came. Three-oh-five pm. Her brother's voice was crackly, distant, despite being only five minutes down the road.

'They're saying it's time,' he said.

By the time Kate had reached high school, her friends' mothers had all returned to work. Helen had remained stubbornly at home. She was always there, fussing at Kate's backpack when she arrived home from school, pulling out newsletters and worksheets, lunch boxes and homework diaries. A fresh cake would be cooling on the kitchen bench, its warm scent intoxicating after an endless day at school.

'I'm on a diet, Mum, I can't eat that. What a waste.'

'Nonsense,' Helen would say, 'eat the cake.'

It was too much. There was always too much Helen, and not enough air to breathe.

The phone calls started the day after it happened. Kate's aunts. Her friends. Helen's friends. And the meals, too. Baskets placed softly on the doorstep with a note inside, next to the apple crumble. So much apple crumble.

'I can feed my family,' Kate told Paul, banging ineffectually at the pots and pans in the kitchen. 'I'm not dead.'

He looked at her warily. Between them, Isabelle sat cheerfully in her highchair, gorging on apple crumble.

Kate was fifteen when her mother fell pregnant with Hugh. A change of life baby, everybody called it. But Kate knew it for what it was—a replacement, an attempt at a less disappointing child. That was when the chest appeared. Helen began to fill it with the baby clothes and blankets that Hugh grew out of, soft woollen items, impossibly small. Helen held each of them to her nose, and then to her breast, before placing them delicately into the box. Presumably, Kate's baby things were in there too, beneath the more recent items for Hugh. Kate never checked. Unbearable to think of looking and finding that she wasn't in there at all.

Baskets of lasagne were falling from the sky. Sticks of garlic bread wrapped in aluminium foil were missiles aimed at her front door. The food avalanched into her foyer, spreading a sickening slick of red sauce along her white tiles. Flowers, too, rained from the ceiling, suffocating her. She was buried alive, weighed down by the cheerful faces of pink dahlias. And then her mother was closing the lid of the cherry oak chest and darkness was descending on

Kate as she crouched, folding herself into an apologetic ball, watching Helen's face shrink and disappear before the dark was permanent. Kate gasped and become aware of Paul's face hovering over hers in the murky dawn light.

'You alright?' he asked, a hand on her leg. 'You were crying.'

Kate saw her mother's eyes again, watching her as the lid came down. She felt the claustrophobia, the impression she was being put in her place.

'A nightmare,' she said. 'Over now.'

'It's time,' she had told Paul. He was asleep, his long back facing her. She'd placed a hand on his shoulder to wake him, the excitement and trepidation making her giddy. Isabelle took a full day and night to arrive, and even after a sweaty, herculean effort, they'd had to cut the baby from her anyway. After Kate was made to wait on the recovery ward for a whole hour—sixty agonising minutes, each one worse than the labour itself, falling like an axe at her ability to endure, her skin tingling with anticipation, with longing—she was reunited with the squawling infant who she pressed to her chest in relief and happiness and grief.

'You're with me now,' she had whispered to Isabelle. 'You're safe with me.'

As a grandmother, Helen was attentive and possessive, lifting Isabelle from Kate's arms, insisting that she go and lie down while Helen held the baby.

At times like this, Kate longed for a sister, someone to whom she could convey the exasperation and resentment: does she ever give up? There was no question of not handing the baby over. Kate would dutifully nestle Isabelle in her grandmother's arms and traipse to her bed, a distorted combination of fury and relief.

Isabelle was one now and the chest had moved in and with it a confusing mixture of irritation, sadness and disbelief.

'She can't go,' she said to Paul after Isabelle had fallen asleep, fattened on apple crumble and custard. 'She's Helen. She's always there. Whether you want her to be not.'

As they prepared for the funeral, Hugh coming over early to deliver wine for the wake, the fact of it sat uncomfortably on Kate's shoulders, like an ill-fitting dress, too tight, too restrictive. Wearing a long, navy dress that Helen would have declared 'appropriate', Kate sat at the edge of her lounge, poised, ready and yet wholly unprepared. A hand touched her on the shoulder.

'It's time to go,' Paul said.

After the service, led by a solemn Church of England rector whose sonorous voice was its own funeral dirge, Kate watched the hearse travel away from her along the pebbly memorial drive. Paul approached, the gravel crunching beneath his feet. He was eating a triangle cheese sandwich and carrying a plastic cup of warm beer.

'Aunt Mavis said she would take the chest off your hands,' he said.

She felt Isabelle at her legs then, clinging and looking upward, whining for her mother. Kate hoisted the toddler onto her hip and fixed her gaze on the black vehicle, turning now onto a paved road and rounding a bend so that Kate could no longer watch its progress. There was rosemary in the air, and the heavy scent of roses, and, on the undercurrent of the breeze, a note of lavender and mothball in a neat silk bag.

'Tell her she can't have it,' she said.

Nebula

Mike Morell

Dad's character's name was Wag. Audiences came alive whenever Wag appeared.

He blamed himself. But I can't help feeling it was me.

The Saddest Clown. It pinches me, he's remembered that way.

The night of the fall was particularly steamy. Program sales were high, the audience fanned themselves constantly with them. One of my jobs was to sell them out front before the show. It was a rare chance to interact with non-circus folk.

I'd look out for kids around my age. Mostly, for boys like me. I'd try to imagine their lives, put myself in their shoes. I looked at their faces to figure out which feature I liked most—their smile, eyes, jawline.

One boy stood out that night. It wasn't one thing that made his face particularly beautiful, it was all parts together. He was so happy wandering with his friends, buying fairy floss, playing the clown games. His joy shined and drew me in. I wanted to stare. But when I checked Mum in the ticket booth opposite, her scowling eyes caught mine. I had to be content stealing glances.

When you walked through the curtain, it took a bit for your eyes to adjust. We were trained not to blink; it broke the glamour illusion. You had to jut your chin upward and count each step. It was a necessary torment. Under the floods and sweeping spots, sequins sparkled, teeth flashed, and glitter cannons dazzled. Dad used to say, 'The ring was a wondrously shiny universe.' Without light, there was no magic.

Our family act was one of the top-billing acts. We were constantly passing each other as we moved between the front and back of the curtain. The motorbike routine, though, was the one time all three of us were together beneath the lights. It involved my parents and I performing a series of balances while riding a circling motorbike. The balances got increasingly difficult, leading to our finale where we all stood atop each other's shoulders. Me on top, then Mum, and Dad at the base driving with his feet.

The most precarious part of the act for me was the middle bit. Dad drove, and Mum sat on his shoulders, arms stretched upward, holding me while I balanced above in a handstand. Upside-down, looping in circles, distracted by lights and faces, I'd struggled for a long time to nail it. I'd assumed it was my mother's pillar-like arms that held me up. Her contrary advice still echoes.

'Focus on your hands, that's what's holding you up. Don't rely on anyone but yourself.'

I didn't want to give her any reason to doubt.

While the circus ring was bright and awe-inspiring, behind the curtain was a den of shadows. The dark concealed the truth, closed it away like a firmly locked closet. 'It was here,' Dad would say, 'where wizards pulled the levers of a carefully constructed Emerald City.'

It had become a habit, whenever I exited the stage, to yank the curtain closed behind me, concealing me in the inky dimness. The adrenalin quickly dissipated. It felt like I was shrinking with each step as I weaved through bodies, brushing up against sweat-slick bums and thighs, back to my own stuffy corner.

Mum slumped in front of her mirror. 'I'm suffocating.'

'Moz ...' Dad tilted his head toward Mum.

She held her black locks up out of the way and stared at herself wordlessly. I went over and unzipped her costume.

She dropped her hair and began peeling. Her back remained turned to me as she struggled out of one glitzy leotard to climb into another. Mum always seemed to darken during her metamorphosis into Nebula. I tried not to take it personally.

'That was one of our best tonight, don' cha reckon?' Dad shot me a wink and pulled Wag's baggy all-in-one costume over the spangly number he wore for our act.

I gave him a tight-lipped smile and checked for Mum's reaction.

Dad sat down and picked up a makeup pencil, ready to put on Wag's face. He glanced at Mum.

'You OK?'

'Yeah I'm OK,' she replied, but huffed anyway. 'Timing was out.'

Dad penciled cartoon eyebrows onto his forehead. The more of Wag he painted on, the bigger his expressions became.

'Naaaah ... I don't think so. When?'

I did an audit of my performance in my mind, searching for a slip-up.

'The Comet pose,' she stated. 'The lift was too early.'

Dad forced a smile and shook his head. 'Really? I didn't notice. From where I was, looked perfect.'

Mum rolled up her costume and tossed it on the ground. 'I shouldn't have said anything.'

'Aww ... come on hun.' Dad put down his pencil and turned to face her. 'We were amazing. You heard them; they were going wild. No one notices a tiny detail like that.'

She took her next costume from off its hanger. 'I noticed.'

She began rolling up her tights, preparing to stretch them over her legs. I watched her face. Her lips were pinched and her forehead tight.

'Here, Mum, let me,' I offered, jumping up to take the costume from her.

Mum's signature act was Tungsten's main drawcard. Nebula was her stage name and it was a given that top billing was hers. The public adored Nebula. They held her on a high pedestal of other-worldly perfection.

Her act was the corde lisse. She would climb a rope, suspended from the rig. At the top, she placed her hand, foot or head through a loop attached to the rope, then hung, suspended way above the audience. Dad would be down the bottom. He'd hold the rope and spin it, in large circles, sending Mum flying, faster and faster. For her finale she would spin, with one foot in the loop while holding fireworks and showering the ring in tiny golden stars.

Her costume was stunning; a black bodysuit covered head to toe in exquisite precious stones—black opals. It took a delicate touch to put it on. I held the leg holes open as she dipped her pointed toes inside. The gems tinkled as we pulled it over her body's contours. You had to be vigilant because beads occasionally snagged and had to be released before they pulled.

When it was on, I stood back for Mum to inspect herself in the mirror. She turned this way and that, checking every inch. Her shimmer was mesmerising, even in the backstage gloom.

Mum froze. She sucked a sharp intake of air through her teeth.

I snapped out of my trance.

Dad turned his head sharply. 'What's wrong?'

Mum held her arm up and touched a spot just beneath her armpit. 'Look.'

There was a gap. A bead or two were missing.

'Sorry Mum,' I said. It wasn't me, but I felt I should apologise anyway.

'Have you got a needle?' Dad asked. 'Slip your arm out, I'll fix it up real quick.'

'Don't be silly. You've got to be back on stage in a minute.'

She yanked open the dresser drawer and shoved its contents around.

'Hey, hey …' Dad said, trying to placate.

She found the sewing kit. Opened and poked at it. Dad placed his hand on her arm. She faced him with a scowl.

'I've got time,' he said. 'All the time in the cosmos, if it means making Nebula complete.'

He picked up the sewing kit to find himself a needle.

During the last two acts, I would sneak beneath the stands and watch from there. The audience were unaware I was lurking in the dark below, peering between their feet. I wasn't performing in either act, so it was okay as long as I could sprint back in time for the curtain call.

Wag was in both acts. Throughout the show, he searches for a way to join in. The performers make a big show of being sceptical. Nevertheless, every act accepts his offers to take part. And without fail, Wag stuffs up every time.

It took a lot of skill to look so bad. Not only did Dad have to be a master of slap stick, but also of the skills each act required. Wag was the backbone of the show. He tied it all together. Dad always said, 'The circus is a glossy pantheon of gods, and in it, a clown represents mere mortal humans.' The audience saw themselves In Wag's imperfection. He commanded their emotions like a conductor flicking a baton, cueing them to feel joy, fear, sorrow or amazement.

The second-last act was the Pointer Twins, Annie and Bonita—knife-throwers. In a final attempt to prove himself, Wag convinces them to take him on as their assistant. A flurry of bumbling gags follows—trips, bumps, mix-ups and chases—ending with Wag knocking the giant wheel Annie is strapped to off its axel, sending it spinning across the stage, forcing Bonita to peg knives at her sister as she rolls out of the ring. By this point, the audience are in stitches.

Just as the laughter and applause starts to wane, Wag wanders into the centre of the ring, head down and arms hanging limp. Bonita marches up to him and gives him a blasting. She tells him he is useless, pathetic and has no place in the circus. The floodlights dim and Wag is left weeping beneath the spotlight.

The rest of the ring is almost black by now. When someone enters, the audience can see someone approaching but can't make out who it is. A shimmering arm reaches into the circle of light and a hand is placed on the broken clown's shoulder.

Wag staggers back a few paces. His knees buckle. He clutches his heart. He looks to the audience, imploring them to assure him the vision is real. Nebula steps forward. With her thumbs, she wipes away his tears, leaving smudged streaks across his makeup. She removes his wig and flings it to the ground. Her rope descends into the spotlight's shaft. She reaches up, grabs it, and holds it out for him to take.

I had probably seen the act a thousand times. I rarely watched it anymore. Instead, I watched the audience's faces. There was just enough light bouncing off their skin to reveal their expressions. Alone, in the dark, it was my guilty pleasure.

I scanned the crowd for one person in particular. The boy with the beautiful face.

He sat rigidly. Both arms straight by his sides and his fingers gripping the front of his bench. His head tilted as he followed Nebula's climb to the apex of the tent. Shadows slid away and a soft glow bathed his perfect face. I watched him freely. Without anyone watching me. He was fully invested in the unfolding story and through him I saw every detail of it anew.

Like Nebula, I wanted to smooth away his fears. I traced his skin with my eyes instead of my thumbs. I felt all his emotions—concern, relief, delight. And, when Nebula reached her finale and the cascading fireworks lit up his face—rapture.

As if a switch had been flipped, the boy's expression changed. The audience let out a collective gasp. Gazes dropped from the top of the tent to the floor.

The spell broke. I was beneath the stands again.

They reeled back, hard against their seats. Eyes and mouths opened wide. Then they were on their feet, straining to get a view. It was near impossible to see past them into the ring. Just momentary glimpses of people running from backstage, bunching in the middle, and in the centre of it all—Wag on his knees and Nebula in his arms.

The spotlight continued to shine. The rope swung limply in its column.

My face flushed hot. No one knew I was there, but it felt like every eye was on me.

Someone turned off the light.

The ring went black.

Nest Egg
Alison Lloyd

Rosie's new landlord had a pleasant, educated voice with a faint, foreign clip to his consonants. He was nothing like the hoary old retirees she was used to in owners. Only a bit older than herself, he had an elegant Asiatic slant to his eyes, fine-grained skin and plentiful hair looped back in a silky plait.

His rental was advertised as 'cosy'. It was a converted bus, an ex-motorhome with a dead motor, sheltering under a Japanese maple at the back of his house. Inside the bus, retro passenger seats cupped a tiny table. A kitchen bench parallel parked across the aisle. The only luxury was the quantity of autumn sun pouring through windows on three sides.

The landlord was almost apologetic. 'It's—um—functional.'

'Yes,' she agreed. She could pay for somewhere bigger but she was trying to save. Not for a house deposit, like she should, but for her dream trip to Spain. Or Nepal. Or anywhere with exotic vistas.

'I'll take it.'

The young landlord offered his hand to shake. He seemed energetic and purposeful, she thought. His black plait made him look aristocratic, like a Manchu prince she'd seen in some film. She could picture him in knee-high curled-toe boots, striding through snow on a mission for the Emperor.

'Joe,' he said.

His name was more ordinary than she expected.

'Z-H-O-U. I go by Joe. Easier for Anglos.'

He checked out her shoes, she noticed. Might be one of those men who liked heels. Or it could be because, to let him know she had an income, she told him she worked in footwear.

'Doesn't everyone?' he quipped.

She laughed and explained about the boutique. He told her he managed his family's restaurants. 'Lot of unsociable hours,' he told her. 'Late nights, weekends.'

Zhou also introduced his uncle, who shared the house. 'The chef.'

He was an older, imperial version of Zhou, whose eyebrows slanted like the eaves of a Buddhist temple. He didn't speak much English.

Rosie was vaguely sorry she didn't see much of the landlord after she moved in, except for the occasional wave. So she didn't ask permission for the extra tenants of his backyard. She'd thought it was a brilliant idea, giving her nephews real, fertilised eggs for Easter. Until the five hatched chicks grew big enough to climb out of the incubator and plop on her sister's carpet. Her sister drove the whole cheeping boxful round to the bus—on a Saturday afternoon when Zhou was out. The rental ad hadn't specified 'no pets'.

Rosie bought a second-hand coop and painted it to look like a Swiss chalet, heart motifs and all. It took a bite out of the nest egg, but what else should she do with the chicks? Besides, she'd fallen in love with them. Adorable puff balls, the lot. A couple of white silkies, two gorgeously marbled Pekins and an odd-chicken-out with glossy midnight plumage. They were exotic, and a balm to her heart, after last year's breakup. She christened them 'la famiglia'.

She watched them through the window, foraging in a gracious dance— scrape, scrape, bow and peck—like a set of court ladies in fluffed dresses and feathery knickerbockers. The black one was bigger and bossier than the rest. She called it the Don, head of the family. A Facebook group said they might start to lay soon.

The knock on the bus door caught her by surprise.

Zhou's cologne wafted over as she folded back the door. He was in leather dress shoes, chinos, and a tailored linen shirt—a date, she thought. Although he seemed weary.

'Erm, can I ask a favour?'

'Sure,' she said brightly.

He waved his mobile phone. 'Could you take a video? My uncle always cuts off my head.'

She clattered down the steps and jumped the last bit to the ground. Zhou grabbed her arm to steady her.

'Careful,' he said, his hold solicitous. 'My uncle wonders how you work in those.'

'I'm fine,' she said archly. 'Thanks!'

Zhou directed her inside the house. 'Part of the package,' he explained. 'It's for my parents, to show back in Taiwan.'

'They haven't seen it?' The house was new and spacious. Her heels teetered a little on the tiling. Zhou's lovely eyes flicked down to her shoes again.

'What, the house?' he said. 'Yes, they bought it, because they, ah, want me to marry. The video is for—' a blush tinged his cheekbones '—a possible partner.'

She was astonished. He looked—well, Asian, yes—but modern. 'I thought matchmaking was centuries ago,' she said.

The blush deepened and his smile became shy. Surely some girl would fall for that look. Don't go down that track, she advised herself. She concentrated on filming while he gave a tour of the house in Chinese.

'Don't you mind?' she asked, when she offered him back his phone.

'It's not forced marriage.' He shoved the phone in his back pocket. 'I haven't got my act together, so, my family is helping out. Chinese women expect a house.'

She was slightly horrified that he'd acquiesced. 'That's so materialistic,' she protested.

'It's not. It's practical. Families have to live somewhere.'

The chickens chose that moment to fly into a squabble. She could hear them squawking and she flinched.

'Your black hen,' Zhou sighed, 'is a rooster. I only got four hours sleep.'

Don. She'd suspected as much, the way he shepherded the ladies. And because of the big bright coxcomb. But she'd put it down to the breed. She honestly hadn't heard anything in the early hours.

She apologised profusely. 'I'll put a lid on him,' she promised.

'Okay.'

She liked the way his return smile flexed the muscles of his face.

She wasn't sure exactly how to silence the rooster. On the Monday she retrieved a cardboard packing box from the boutique's recycling and took it out into the twilight garden. The birds were roosting, snuggled in a tight row, heads under their wings. They chirruped sleepily at her approach. She crouched, and ducked into the warm and pongy coop. A smooth white egg gleamed like porcelain in the dusk. The first. Beautiful.

Collect that in a minute, she thought. First she grabbed the rooster with both hands and bundled him under the box.

'This is for your own good, chicky. Just for nights, so, cooperate, hey? It's Jimmy Choo, no less.'

Don squawked and batted his wings for a bit, before settling to sleep.

Or so she thought, when she backed out of the coop, egg held safe against her chest. But the rooster must have got flappy because in the morning Jimmy Choo was overturned. The Don was perched victoriously on top. Oh dear. He didn't know what was good for him.

Zhou was at her door the following Saturday, suavely dressed again.

'We need to re-shoot,' he said. 'My uncle reckoned I looked like an idiot. I kept repeating myself because I was tired.'

They went through the house again. Rosie could hear the Don doing his thing outside. Who knew roosters crowed in the afternoon as well? When they'd finished the video, she apologised again about the noise.

'I bought earplugs.' Zhou smiled. 'No problem.'

But there was a problem, Zhou told her next morning. His uncle didn't like the video because the rooster could be heard clearly in the background. 'He says people will think I live in some village backwater.'

Zhou said he'd sent the video anyway. 'Look. I don't want to do the mean landlord thing,' he went on, 'but you said you'd put the rooster in the pot.'

'No, I said I'd put a lid on him. Like—keep him quiet.'

She wrapped her dressing-gown tighter. She didn't have much on underneath.

His gaze fixed on a spot past her ear. 'Well, my uncle's insisting. You'll have to get rid of it.'

'I thought *you* were the owner,' she said.

Zhou folded his arms. 'I am. But I respect my elders.'

He returned to the house. She mooched around making coffee. She thought she heard a raised voice and a door slam. Through the window, the rooster exuberantly hailed the day, his breath spiralling in the cold, while his tail fluttered like a pennant. Her chickens were the one spot of colour in the wintry backyard. Her sister wouldn't take them back, and she couldn't bear to condemn the Don to soup. That would be a betrayal of family, a Godfather-like execution.

She just had to show Zhou's uncle that the chickens were practical, since that obviously mattered to him. He was a chef, wasn't he? She wasn't much of a cook, but what if she gave him fresh, free-range eggs?

She hadn't eaten any because it seemed a shame to break them. She counted —eight perfect eggs, including one slightly bigger than the others. She put them in a bright pink shoebox and tied a ribbon around to dress it up. Then she click-tapped up to the house in her best end-of-season-clearout platforms.

She was disappointed that the uncle opened the door but she offered him the gift. She gushed because she was nervous and his pagoda eyebrows tilted seismically into a frown.

'No chicken,' he said. He guillotined the air with his hand. 'Chicken, or you—go!'

She went. In the bus she sat in a pane of sunlight and scrolled desultorily through rental ads. There wasn't anything cheap within an hour and a half's commute of work. She rang and made a time to see a share house that said it welcomed animals.

She was thinking what to wear for the afternoon appointment when Zhou appeared in an apron, waving.

'Come over!' He looked excited.

She really didn't want to see some girl he'd fallen for. Still, she followed him and the scent of frying shallots to the kitchen, where Zhou's uncle was shaking and swishing a hot wok.

'Uncle says he didn't mean to be rude. He thought you were giving me fancy shoes.'

Zhou the elder gestured to a pair of bowls on the bench. 'Look!' His spatula rang on the wok.

One bowl contained a beaten egg mix. The other held a pair of shiny orange yolks.

'From me?' she asked.

The uncle swirled the mix into the wok and shouted above the sizzle.

Zhou translated. 'The big egg had a double yolk! We call them 'double gold' in Chinese. Really rare! And really good luck. He's inviting you for lunch.'

Zhou looked so hopeful she accepted.

The omelette was melt-in-the-mouth; the conversation less so. Zhou the elder politely invited her to Taiwan, twice.

'I'd like to go,' she said. 'But ...' There were several of those. 'Lunch will have to do me for now. I've got to be going. I'm looking at another place.'

Zhou bit his lip. 'My uncle says I should see you home. He thinks your shoes are dangerous.'

'There's really no need,' Rosie said. She just had to get her handbag.

'Let me.'

He stopped under the maple tree, courteous and slightly embarrassed. 'Rosie—I've had second thoughts. Keep the rooster.'

'Really? But what about the video and all that?' Not that it was any of her business.

'I didn't like her much. You know ...' Zhou's eyes were intense and purposeful. 'You are like your chickens. Cheery, a bit fluttery, and—'

'Decorative? Impractical?'

'*Ke'ai.*' He translated. 'Lovable. The rooster is impractical, but he's worth it for—'

She expected him to say 'fresh ingredients.' But instead he said, 'You.'

'Oh!' She was definitely a bit fluttery.

'Have I—erm—totally missed the bus?'

'The bus isn't going anywhere,' Rosie said. Neither was she, for a while at least. With a touch on her arm Zhou drew her under the maple's canopy. She felt like a chicken come home to roost.

The Don fluffed his flamboyant feathers and crowed in joyous approval.

The Nun

Jenni Mazaraki

The nun watches me.

Headphones in, I'm listening to a song about bodies. A woman sings defiantly about flesh and sweat, of rhythms between bodies, tongues and hands searching while the nun across the tram aisle stares right into my face, into my eyeballs, into my head. My insides stir.

I look away just in case she can see something in me. Then I think about other situations where prolonged eye contact is permitted. Staring competitions (no blinking), when you're flirting in a moment of mutual attraction, when you're held close and holding them right back, slowly falling.

The tram stops and starts. Metal-on-metal screeches, and I look up to see a man who reminds me of someone I used to know sitting near the doorway of the tram gazing at his phone.

It could almost be him. I can almost taste him. In front of all of these people—the early morning yawners, the too loud talkers, the headphone wearers—I feel the urge that pulled me to him all that time ago.

I fumble with my phone and switch to another track that I listened to when I was sixteen. One that we used to listen to together. I wonder if the nun is still looking at me but I don't check. I wonder if she can tell that I am thinking about the first time I felt bare thighs against my own. I wonder if she is judging me or blessing me or just thinking about lunch.

I think about the nun and her neat position. All tidy and tucked up tightly on the tram, knees together. Hands placed gently side by side on top of her black leather bag, it too, neat and small and compact. There is no ring on her finger. *But isn't she married to Jesus, forever?* My thoughts sound childlike to me, as I think about her one and only invisible man. I'm not wearing my ring today either. Left on the windowsill after doing the breakfast dishes.

Is she happy? Has her life brought her contentment? What is it to believe in God and ritual and centuries of structure, handed down by the bible and institutions heavy with stone and expectations?

Is she happy? I am often not very happy at all. With my anxious thoughts, my what-ifs bumping around in my brain and body at a constant, yet surprising rhythm.

I briefly look at the nun and notice the two small crucifixes on each lapel of her pale green shirt collar. What a comfort, I imagine, to feel so secure in your beliefs that you have them sit either side of your throat like lucky charms. A reminder of all that holds you; all that holds your insides in.

No one taught me about God. Except for the lady who came to our primary school each week and taught us songs about Jesus. In the songbooks she gave us, Jesus looked like my next door neighbour, so I assumed he must be okay. My parents believed in things they could see and touch. They believed in things like lawnmowers and roast dinners. Called themselves sensible people, did what they liked to call, sensible things. Reading newspapers, painting fences, washing cars. A cold beer at the end of the working day, a couple more on the weekend.

It was around about the time that we learned a song about Jesus coming back from the dead that I decided to pray every night. I'd lie there in bed, flat on my back in the dark and I would pray to God like I was writing a letter. We'd been taught all about writing letters in class and how it was polite to sign off with *yours sincerely,* so that's what I did, followed by a stern *Amen,* just to seal the deal, to make sure God knew that I was over and out. Just like how my brother and I communicated on our walkie-talkies in the backyard.

If I didn't pray, I knew there would be some kind of trouble.

But my prayers were like wishes for things that I did not need but wanted so very much. Like a slap band or a glitter pen. I told God that I would be good so that I could get these things. I promised. I didn't want Jesus coming back from the dead like a zombie to get me. Like I said, no one taught me about God except for the lady who came each week and made us clap hands to the rhythm. Some of us singing without really knowing why.

The tram sways uncomfortably through a bend and I balance myself in my seat. The nun appears unperturbed, as though she possesses some internal mechanism that keeps her steady and grounded.

Outside the grimy window, the flower clock. Even first thing in the morning, tourists are taking each other's photos in front of it. This path is familiar but everything is different. Back then, I travelled down this road in my school uniform, sick to my stomach about the day that lay in wait for me once I walked through the school gates. Rules and bells and fitting in. Those days are gone. I'm now in my thirties, listening to music from the time I loved a boy at school. A boy who told me I was beautiful and whose kisses tasted like salt and vinegar chips. I'm travelling down St Kilda Road with my phone held tightly in my hands. My phone is filled with photos of my children—at the park, finger painting, holding the cat and I'm thinking about who I used to be.

Everything is different now. I watch the man on the tram, see his hands with neatly clipped fingernails. I see his throat with the Adam's apple protruding and I remember my high school boyfriend's throat that I once licked and sucked and tasted. I involuntarily remember the smell of him behind his ears, the feel of his jeans, the way his bed sagged under the weight of the two of us.

Everything is different now, and I wonder where he is, how his life turned out. I watch the man on the tram move his backpack and remember my high school boyfriend, our bodies pressing against each other in awkward teenage poses. I don't want to remember but it pushes at me anyway. I wonder if he goes about his day and sometimes remembers my body, the one that I agonised about, that body strong with feeling. My waist still remembers his grip.

I remember it all of a sudden and I don't want to remember. I am surprised that my body feels without intention.

In peak hour traffic, the music blares into my ears, damaged with tinnitus from those nights in dark corners next to loud speakers. I might want to forget, but my body remembers fragments of myself. I remember the songs that played when we kissed for hours.

I don't believe we have soulmates or unique connections, just moments with people. I remember that he was never mine when he was mine.

In high school, my boyfriend's family had a picture of Jesus in the hall. They taught me how to say grace, tried to save my soul. In our hall was a funny cartoon that Dad had cut out of the newspaper and put in a metal picture frame. Something about a duck playing cricket.

We met on the oval. The grass had recently been mown and it had been raining. I brushed my bare arm against his as I walked past and kept going. I didn't need to look back to know he was watching. The first time alone in his bedroom, he talked about flowers and purity and gift. I told him to stop talking, just, stop, talking—but keep going.

In his room we were together but he wouldn't hold my hand in public. Slipped against each other's skin and one time fell off the bed, landing together in a wet splat on his beanbag. I'd never felt like that, didn't know my body could do those things and I wanted more. I would have swallowed him whole and collapsed in after him and stayed there forever, but there was school and homework and the real world outside of his room. And, anyway, his parents got home from work at the usual time each day, first his mum, then his dad by the time dinner was ready.

Gave me chills when he kissed me but told me not to tell anyone about us. Our secret love. I'd help him make his bed and open the window to let our heat out of the small space before his mum got home. *You're insatiable*, he'd whisper to me as I slid my hand down his jeans when his mum had her back turned, placing a quiche, or pie in the oven.

Said he'd like me a bit thinner, a bit blonder, a bit something else.

At home in bed at night I stopped talking to God and started rehashing conversations with my boyfriend in my head instead. He talked about the day when I made enough changes and we could be together—*properly together*. I stopped wishing for things I did not need.

The nun stands to get off at her stop. I meet her gaze and hold it until she looks away. I see her scuffed shoes, her half smile, her shoulders held at an angle. I change the tune.

Set In Stone

Tina Morganella

They stood leaning on the railing at the very start of the jetty. He kept his hands in his pockets, she kept brushing the hair back from her face, the wind wreaking havoc. She turned her back on the sea and admired instead, the lofty angles of the mountains. What had looked like snow turned out to be the striking scars of excavation.

'So that's where the Carrara marble comes from, eh?' Sandra said. The town of Massa Carrara lay low and flat underneath. Red tiled apartments spread far down the coast. 'I suppose one day it's going to run out.'

'I think there's plenty still. The whole mountain range!' Stefano replied, with a sweep of his hand. They stared at it silently.

'Thank you,' she said suddenly. 'For lunch, for everything.'

'No problem. Thank you for coming. It's really good to see you.'

'I thought it might be a bit weird. It's been, what … 10 years I think?'

'A long time!'

'It's fine, though, isn't it?' And it had been. When she had emailed to ask if she could visit, she convinced herself that it was just to seek out a familiar face in a foreign land. She was travelling through Italy alone and knew that she would soon enough crave company. They had been close once. He had immediately responded that she should come, absolutely. There was the odd update—she knew he was married with a son—but they hadn't seen each other in person since he left Australia and returned to his birthplace.

That normality quickly faded though, as soon as they were alone on the jetty. Stefano's wife Amelia was down on the sand with their son. She looked up at them now, shielding the sun with her hand and waved at them. They both waved back, silently. Stefano and Sandra alternately admired the sea and mountains, avoiding each other in between.

'They say Michelangelo used to come and pick a block himself,' Stefano said.

'Do you think that's true?'

He shrugged. 'Why not?'

Sandra turned to face him but followed his gaze down to his wife and son instead. 'She's really lovely. Sweet.' Amelia was formed generously—wide hips, big grin, large smiling eyes, a mass of blond hair. She could see why men would find her curves attractive. Or maybe comforting, safe. Stefano instead was a rake, angular and hard, thin straight lines. His dark eyes were friendly only when he wanted them to be.

'She saved me, you know.' Stefano nodded towards Amelia, his eyes half closed against the sharp sun.

'Saved you how?'

'Well. I started doing some bad things when I came back. Not really, really bad, but bad. I couldn't find work. I lost a lot of weight. I was getting involved … you know how I went to South America for a while … and … it was bad. A dark road. When I met her, she helped me find a normal job—her uncle's factory. It's hard labour for not much money, but it's a good job. A good honest job. She took care of me.'

Sandra was surprised. 'Oh. Ok. I didn't realise. She's a good person then.' She meant it. It was clear Amelia was without guile. A decent woman, a good mother. Someone with the strength and enough belief in her God to save someone.

Sandra wondered if she was allowed to ask what 'bad' really meant.

'Actually. I was thinking about coming back to Australia then, but Amelia fell pregnant.' He glanced at Sandra quickly. She bit her lip. 'She wanted to get married. So I stayed here.'

Sandra tried to smile encouragingly, but knew it was fixed and grim. She kept her eyes on the stark mountain scars, following the lines of rupture. She admitted to herself that it hadn't just been company she sought. Her memories of Sydney had led her here. Just to see, just to know how it all worked out, just to find out if he still laughed devilishly, if he still played music, and if he ever sold his screenplay. She didn't expect anything, nothing at all. She knew he had a family. She certainly didn't expect any admissions, not now. Her stomach ached. The seafood she normally never ate still swam, alive, in her stomach. 'Felice is a gorgeous little boy. He's got your smile. How old is he now?'

'Only 7. But he's so smart, so quick already. He's my life.'

They both watched Felice for a moment. He skipped along the sand like a grasshopper, racing ahead, stopping abruptly to pick up something, inspect it and throw it out to sea. His mother followed close behind. The beach was a crowded crosshatch of umbrellas and lounge chairs, but close to the shore Felice could run and play freely.

The sea was grey and vast, despite the summer sun. Far away it was romantic and beautiful. It was only up close, lapping at your feet, that it suddenly became callous and jealous, insistent. Sandra felt the nausea wash over her like the waves. She hesitated, then asked, 'So, you were planning on coming back to Australia then? And now?' The cramp in her stomach twisted in on itself. She added quickly, 'Is Amelia interested? Would she be willing?'

Stefano shook his head. 'No. She said she's scared of flying. Of going so far, leaving her family. As if it was still the old days and they could only write letters.' He laughed with surprising bitterness. 'Felice—he would love it. He would know English faster and better than any of us. You know Felice means happy?'

'Yes, of course. Beautiful name.' She pictured Felice chasing white tipped waves at Palm Beach, nestled safely under lush national park instead of menacing marble. 'So, you'll stay in Italy then.'

'Sì, Sandra. But ... it's hard. All I do is manual labour. It's hard work. I get home and I'm tired. We don't see many friends. I don't make films. I help Felice with his homework and he makes me happy. Amelia is a good woman, a good wife. But I can't get ahead here.'

'You're not writing then?'

He laughed and shook his head. 'No Sandra. No writing. Not in Italian, not in English.'

'I understand. It's hard—you've got a family, you have to make a living. There's not a lot of time to dream and think.'

He shook his head again, but without laughing. 'No, no. It's because I'm stupid. I'm just a stupid Italian man.' He looked straight at her for the first time and twisted his mouth angrily. 'I'm stupid for a lot of reasons. I should never have left.' He stood with his hands gripping the jetty railing. 'First of all, I was free in Australia. No tradition, no rules about how to live. Australians make their own futures, they decide how they do things. They don't have centuries old barriers, expectations. I could breathe clear air there.'

'Second,' Stefano gazed at her intently, 'second, I should never have left you. I was free with you too. We understood each other.'

Her face flushed with heat, and she tried to make light of it. 'I don't think I would've 'saved' you Stefano. Maybe the opposite!' Her voice was too stretched, the tone contrived. It was too painful to return his gaze. She hadn't expected this.

'I wasn't in trouble then. Only when I came back here.'

She looked up at him for just a moment, both of their faces tense, they're bodies stiff and uncomfortable. She wondered if she should tell him but she had promised herself she wouldn't. What use would it be? How he could have had an Australian son. How she kept it secret because he'd already left. How she didn't have the courage to be a mother without him and didn't go through with it. How she thought of it every single day because she'd never had the chance to be a mother again since. Her and Stefano were never anything real, nothing serious. He was always going to leave.

Neither of them had noticed that Amelia and Felice had left the beach and made their way onto the jetty.

'*Papa*', *guarda*!' Felice ran to his father and chattered excitedly about his new collection of shells. Stefano ruffled his son's dark hair and smiled down at him. Then he squatted down and caught him up in a big hug and started examining his collection.

Amelia came up behind him, carrying his hat, his shoes, smiling but tired. Her shoulders drooped, and she shifted her weight from one foot to the other. Her face was hot, her brow damp. Suddenly Sandra felt ashamed that she had taken up their whole Sunday, and that standard etiquette had dictated that they pay for a lunch that, she felt sure now, was beyond their means.

'He's adorable Amelia, you must be very proud of him,' Sandra said in Italian. Amelia didn't speak much English at all.

Amelia beamed. 'Sometimes he's a little cheeky, but otherwise he's a good boy.' Felice squealed in indignation and then shucked his head, grinning but suddenly shy.

'Thanks so much for a wonderful day. I think it's time to go to the train station now,' Sandra said.

Stefano looked at her puzzled. 'I thought it was not until later?'

'Oh no, you must have misunderstood. It leaves in the next hour.'

'Are you sure? Is everything ok?' he asked her in English.

'Yep, everything is just fine.'

They were conscious of avoiding all eye contact now, of causing unnecessary concern for Amelia, who neither of them wanted to hurt.

'Ok, then, we'll drive you into town.'

'Thank you, that would be great.'

Felice asked her in Italian, 'Are you going now? But you're coming back?'

'Oh sweetie, I don't think I will be back. But maybe when you're a bit bigger you can come and visit me in Australia. What do you think?'

His eyes grew wide and he opened his mouth in surprise. He looked up at his mother. *'Possiamo?'*

Amelia squeezed his arms as she shrugged her shoulders. *'Chi sa?'* Who knew, indeed. She kept squeezing until he yelped and struggled out of her grip. He skittered off towards the car, and she quickly followed.

Sandra paused for a moment to take one last look at the mountains. Their endurance was transferred into art, into architecture. Things set in stone. But she understood that nothing lasts forever.

Stefano and Sandra walked side by side in silence to the car. In the station carpark, she exchanged hugs and kisses with the whole family. Stefano was polite but distant, their kiss rushed and deliberately unceremonious. Sandra knelt down to give Felice a big hug. She felt his fragile body flutter against her. He had taken to her and she was glad, even though she knew he would quickly forget her. She smoothed his long dark fringe away from his face. She told him in Italian to be good for mum and dad, and not to be too cheeky. He grinned at her and kissed her again, before hiding behind his mother.

Sandra insisted that they all leave at once and not come inside—she had robbed them of enough time. Then she sat on the platform bench to wait for a train that wouldn't arrive for hours, and quietly cried.

From Where They Came
Michelle Wright

All night, the slash of rifle shots hacked the heavy silence and bounced between the steep, bare, rocky walls. From the village that cowered in a flattened cleft above the narrow canyon, it was impossible to say from where they came—left or right, above or below, and if they were far away or near.

With the first light of day, the people of the village gathered in front of the old Spanish church and then, in single file, began to descend the stone-covered slope towards the bottom of the gorge where they'd been told a bus would be waiting to take them away to safety. In the pale grey of dawn, the path down to the dry creek bed glowed a faded yellow. It slipped and skidded under their hurrying feet like a carpet of dried corn kernels.

Each of the villagers carried as much as they could bear to take, as little as they could bear to leave behind. An old man with a pole across his shoulders, woven bags attached at either end, filled with cans of food and clothes; a middle-aged father bent in two beneath the weight of the small refrigerator he balanced on his back, his chest trickling sweat beneath his open checkered shirt; an old woman leaning on a carved and crooked walking stick, a lighted candle melting in her other hand, wax dripping down her knuckles and trickling between the thick deep veins. Running to keep up with her mother and older siblings, a girl of two or three—a small brown and white chicken clasped to her chest, its head bobbing like an old stuffed toy with each wobbly, clomping step. Most of the people in the line carried small white flags of surrender. They waved them above their heads with every stride they took.

The last person to leave was a young father. He carried nothing, his cheeks slack and flushed with fear. He ran to catch up with the others, his empty hands grasping at their shoulders.

'Have you seen Felipe?' he cried. 'Have you seen my son?'

He ran from person to person and each one shook their head and sighed.

Ever since his mother died, the boy had been a roamer—wandering off to quiet places, climbing trees, disappearing in the morning and coming home at dusk. Before it had not been of great concern. But now, with the shootings and the kidnappings, they all knew that times had changed. They promised to look out for him on their way down the hill. 'He'll be alright,' they said, though their real thoughts they did not say aloud.

The father ran back up towards the village. He left the path, wove between trees and bushes, calling *Mijo! Mijo!'*—'My son! My son!'

When his sister-in-law came searching, she found him seated in the doorway of his house, his hands around his head.

'He's probably gone without you,' she said. 'Don't worry. I'm sure that he'll be waiting at the bus.'

'What if he isn't there?' replied the father.

'He will be,' she said. 'Come with me. Please.'

'You can't be sure. Maybe he's looking for me. Or for that damned book of his. He said he couldn't find it. He said he lost it yesterday.'

'Which book?' asked the sister-in-law.

'I don't know what it's called,' said the father. 'His mother gave it to him for his birthday last year.' He lifted his head towards the low-clouded sky, stretched his throat and swallowed a mouthful of warm, dry air. 'The last birthday,' he said.

The woman took her brother-in-law by the elbow.

'Come,' she said. 'We can't stay here. We have to go. My girls are alone on the bus. It won't wait. Please come quickly. We'll see if he's there.'

When they arrived at the road, all the other people from the village were already on the bus. The woman's eldest daughter was kneeling on her seat, the top half of her body squeezed through an open window.

'Mamá,' she cried. 'Why did you take so long? I thought you weren't coming back.'

'Is your cousin on the bus?' asked the mother.

The girl frowned, shook her head, her pigtails flicking left and right against the window frame. 'No, he's not here. I haven't seen him since we left home.'

The woman turned to her brother-in-law as the bus driver started the engine.

'I'm so sorry,' she said. 'I wish I could stay with you, but I have to take the girls to safety.' She clasped his shoulders and kissed him on the cheek. 'Be careful, please.'

The father stood by the open door of the bus, his hand gripping the metal handle, his arm straight and tense as if he could keep it there with the force of his aching muscles.

Through an open window, the little girl with the chicken stared down at him. Her lips were pressed against the chicken's head and she mouthed the words of a song. In the half-heard syllables, the father recognised an ancient lullaby so old his grandma sang it for him.

'Arrorró mi niño. Arrorró mi sol.' Her voice was low and calm for such a small child, like the purring of a cat, and the father's eyes grew heavy with the sleepless night he'd spent.

Suddenly, from above, came the hollow *ping ping ping* of bullets as they struck a rocky surface. The man jumped as the driver of the bus yelled out to him.

'Get in or I'll leave you here!'

The father strained his ears, trying to detect from where the sound of bullets was coming, but the echo was smothered by the noise of the motor as the bus started up and pulled away. The father turned his head and raised his eyes in the direction of his home. Far above on the gravelled path a figure ran down towards the road. Its skidding, stumbling feet raised a veil of dirt, the sun reflecting off the particles, forming golden whorls that lifted and were carried away in the dislocated air behind the moving body. As the figure drew nearer, the father was sure it was a young child. He squinted against the glare of the morning sun, but couldn't be sure it was his boy. The child was running down the hill, his head bent forward, eyes cast downwards to avoid the jagged stones protruding here and there. The dust that his shoes lifted tumbled and grew as he ran, forming a cloud that hid his feet. One scrawny, ochre arm was extended in front of his chest, holding a stick with a piece of white paper attached. Over his shoulder, he carried a white plastic bag. It didn't appear to have anything in it, as if he hadn't found what he was looking for. As the boy ran, the bag filled with air and emptied, fluttering up and falling back against his shoulder blades with each uncertain bound. Suddenly, from the walls of the narrow gorge, came the crack of bullets. The father gasped, then clenched his teeth so hard he thought they would crumble. He pressed both hands over his ears and held his breath. He searched the dusty, yellow path until he found the boy. On the steep slope, for several seconds, the child appeared to soar, then slipped and staggered, his arms thrown back, the plastic bag billowing behind him. In the pale morning light, he seemed, just for a moment, like a broken angel falling back to earth.

Splinter

James Turvey

Everyone calls my uncle Splinter, or Splint for short, because he's so skinny. My sister, Terry, and I have come to visit him with Dad.

Splinter lives right on the Georges River, a stone's throw from East Hills pub; Dad's old stomping ground. The house is built high up on stilts to avoid the tide and the space below it is filled with reeds so high that they tickle the floorboards from below.

'Riddled with brown snakes under there,' Dad says as we climb the wooden stairs to the door. 'That's why the dogs have to live inside.'

We don't knock, Dad just opens the front door and yodels 'ayooooo' as we enter, always playing the cowboy.

The stench of dogs hits us before the actual dogs do. They struggle through the putrid air as their claws slip and slide on the wooden hall to meet us. They're Shar Pei crosses, heads like the Purex Toilet Paper dogs from telly, but on steroids. They butt into us and the slime oozing from their mouths leaves snail trails on our clothes.

'Ayaaaah,' Dad shouts, more cowboy talk, this time as if he's wrangling horses. The dogs seem to understand him and they skid back up the hallway.

We follow Dad out onto the balcony where Splinter has his living quarters.

'The rest of the house belongs to the dogs,' Splinter says, and I'm not sure if he means it figuratively or literally or both.

This is the first time I've clapped eyes on Splinter in twenty-five years. He'd visited us once when we first moved to Newcastle. He rode in on a Triumph and stayed as long as it takes to drink a coffee.

'It's a wonder the rat is strong enough to hold on,' Mum had said as he rode off.

Although Dad is lean, his tattoos sit on muscle; Splinter's sit on bone. He has a moustache and wears thick glasses with gold rims that magnify his eyes behind the lenses like a cartoon character.

The blue Bonds singlet he wears is meant to hug the skin, but it hangs from his frame; Dad's white t-shirt fits him well.

No hellos are spoken, no catching up or how have you been; instead he points to the fridge at the far end of the balcony.

'Beers are in there if you want one.'

The fridge is filled with longnecks of Tooheys New; some laying on their sides, some standing up, some in the door where normal people would keep milk and juice. Surely a case of twist tops or cans would make more sense. Getting up less is all I can come up with.

I take three and hand them out, Splinter already has one.

Dad crushes his bottle cap in half after he twists it off. I do it instinctively whenever I open a beer too. We have the same hands, but his have done more labour, seen more sun and a couple of his knuckles sit in the wrong spots. It's the first time I've thought about it and I wonder what else I've inherited from him too.

All the furniture is made of bamboo and with the river running right there in front of us it's like we're on the set of *Gilligan's Island*. There's a shelving unit against the side wall with a small TV on the top shelf that wouldn't look out of place if it was made of coconuts. The bamboo daybed that Splinter sits on has a pillow and sleeping bag at one end, which makes me think he wasn't joking about the dogs.

Dad motions for Terry to take a seat on the single bamboo stool. The large beer in her hand dwarfs her. She smiles up at me as Dad and Splinter discuss the horses they've backed, when they got up and how much they won. There's no mention of how much they've lost or how much they're down by.

Down below us and to the left is the East Hills Footbridge that goes from this side of the river over to Voyager Point. When Mum was a teenager, she'd take her horse across the bridge and explore the bushland around the migrants' camp on the other side.

There's more to the footbridge though, and I'm waiting for Dad to tell us, because I know he can't help himself. I've heard the story from Mum a hundred times, but never from his lips. Terry probably doesn't know this one though, she let it be known a long time ago that her quota for violence was full.

I pass Splinter another longneck from the fridge when he finishes the one he's on and he doesn't make eye contact with me, maybe because I'm bigger than him or because he lives on a veranda or because Mum thinks he's a rat.

'See the footbridge?' Dad says, taking a swig of his beer.

Here it comes.

'Me and your old girl were looking for somewhere to be alone, you know?'

'Oh yeah?' Splinter laughs.

'Not like that, ya grub,' Dad gives Splinter a little kick in the shin that uncrosses his legs for him.

'We'd come down to the water to smoke a joint, but the tide was right up to the bank. There was nowhere to sit, so Deli says she knows of a spot on the other side of the bridge.'

Dad stops here, takes one of Splinter's smokes and throws the box back onto his lap. There's a breeze coming in off the water and he does that thing where he cups his hands around the cigarette to light it. He takes a big drag and stares at the lit tip in confusion as he breathes out.

'What the fuck are these?'

'Dunhills.'

'They taste like shit.'

'Bring ya fuckin' own then next time.'

'Don't fuckin' swear at me in front of my kids.'

'Can you just get on with the fucking story?' Terry says.

Dad and I laugh and she laughs too. Splinter just shakes his head and drinks more beer.

'Righto, righto. It was dark and we're about a quarter of the way across before we notice two blokes up ahead, sitting either side of the bridge. They've got their legs out like smartarses, trying to block the way. Deli grabs my hand, because she's scared and we're not looking for trouble.'

'You were always looking for trouble,' Splinter interrupts.

'Well, I would've preferred to smoke a joint with my missus without a blue. She hadn't really seen me go off my rocker yet, just heard stories, y'know?'

'As we get closer I can see their boots, their jackets and haircuts, fuckin' Sharpies, but younger than me. One of them says, 'Nice night,' and I agree and say, 'Yeah, it has been so far,' and we step over their legs casually. As we do, one of them slips his hand up Del's skirt and grabs her arse. I didn't actually see it, but she let out a little yelp and clenched my hand tighter.

'For a second she thought I hadn't noticed because I took another couple of steps, just to get her clear of them. I asked her calmly if one of them had just grabbed her, but she didn't reply.

'What are you gunna fuckin' do anyway?' One of them answered for her.

'I pulled him onto his feet by the collar of his jacket and it was only then that I could see he was lucky to be fifteen.'

'I don't want to hear the rest of it,' Terry says. 'I can figure it out from here.'

'No, trust me, you'll like this one,' I assure her.

'So I lift up him by the collar so we're face to face and he's gotta be about eight stone ringing wet. It's not as if I'm the biggest prick around, either. Before I could do anything, the slippery cunt slides out of his jacket, side steps me and jumps straight over the railing and into the river!'

The four of us all laugh, Terry out of relief more so than anything else.

'It's not exactly a short fall,' she adds looking out at the bridge from the balcony.

'Gotta be twenty-five, thirty feet,' Splinter says, looking into the mouth of his beer with one eye.

'He was swimming for it, boots and all. Deli and I couldn't believe it, not to mention his mate that's been left for dead. Then she goes, 'Well, what are you fuckin' waiting for?' and he jumps over as well!'

We're all laughing again now and Dad takes a long pull of his cigarette and smiles to himself.

'Your mum always had a lot of go in her, I just didn't know it then,' he says, but quieter and not to us, he's thinking out loud.

Dad, Terry and Splinter have one more longneck each as we sit around and make small talk in the wake of the story. I'm still nursing the first one, conscious of having to drive, to escape this place and get Terry home safely.

Splinter doesn't say much, just sits there with a shit-eating grin on his face.

Before we leave I ask Splinter if I can take photos of his tattoos because I'm interested in that kind of thing. He has tattoos by the same people as Dad; Big Pete from over near the train line and Greg Ardron who owned Sleeve Masters in The Cross.

Splinter is suspicious but agrees. There's a parrot on a branch, and the lines are all blown out. The black ink has turned that dark blue colour that old tats get after years in the sun. It looks great like that though, better than it would have new and it's wasted on someone like my uncle.

At the top of his right arm, where the leathered skin hangs down around his bony shoulder socket, there's a naked woman in a martini glass. Her legs hang over the side and behind her are the four aces from a deck of cards. A banner across the glass reads 'Man's Ruin'.

For the first time, I see the irony of it. Women aren't responsible for this pissed old fart. I try to imagine what a 'Woman's Ruin' tattoo would look like. In Mum's case there'd be some fists, a bong and some blank space where Dad should've been.

By the time I finish taking photos, which only takes a minute, Splinter is pretty much asleep and it's our cue to leave.

Dad takes the longneck that's leaning against his brother's chest and places it on the bamboo stool. It's the closest thing to affection that I've seen between them.

Even though I'll imagine it as such whenever I write about it, this is the last time I'll have a view of the Georges River from here and it's the last time that the four of us will ever be in the same place together.

Tent
Susan Bennett

It's Friday evening and they're shopping in an outer suburb, which seems exotic. Later, when she lives there, the same suburb will feel like the ends of the earth. She will be repulsed by the local equivalent of an Easter Parade—buffoons with a can of beer in one hand, promenading their pit bull terriers through the car park on the end of a rope.

But that is not tonight. Tonight, this suburb, with its frenetic, three lane highway, seems a gateway to freedom places. They eat dinner in a near empty pizza joint and this too, with its American-style booths, seems somewhat cosmopolitan even if the pizza is lousy. A flower vendor nears their table carrying a basket filled with cellophane-wrapped red roses. To spare her beau this blackmail, she quickly says, oh no. No, thank you. She is so pleased with herself for not needing a flower, but the restaurant's only other customer, a drunk puffing a cigarette calls, oh go onnnnnnnn, buy the lady a flowerrrrr.

After dinner, they look at tents. In these heady days of new love, he wants to know who will pay for this tent?

She says, I thought we'd go halves.

In these heady days of new love, he wants to know, what happens if we split up?

In the end, he pays for a portable gas stove, she pays for the tent.

Their first trip together, he tells her of another trip with his father, when they took off for parts unknown after the old man consulted the sky looking for fair weather and declared they would head where the sun was shining.

His parents call one another Mum and Dad. Mum tells one story over and over again: how she rescued some half-drowned peafowl from the rain and put them in the warming oven of the wood stove. When she opened the door they were flapping about, brought back to life. His mother pronounces 'says' SAZE but will tell anyone who'll listen that it's peafowl, not peacocks.

Decades later, trawling the internet for news of him she learns that, after the bushfires, the survivors wrote a town history book. Within its pages he accepts medals for fire-fighting and gazes delightedly upon an infant daughter swaddled in a lacy christening blanket. She tries to work out how long between herself and his wife, how many months between his greeting card in the letterbox consigning her to past tense and his marriage.

His sister paints life on the farm as kittens born in haystacks and puppies born in rustic sheds, pumpkins grown beneath majestic, starlit skies, horses ridden through ancient forests. Amid the bravery medals and idyll, nobody speaks of the puppies and kittens they drowned in a bucket. How no one would talk to her after she insisted they spay the dog instead of killing her pups. (More than the dog's worth, said his father. And spayed bitches get fat, he said). No one mentions that the horse died for want of a vet. Or the nights around the campfire when men described ideal women with flat heads to rest beer cans on while they went down on their knees. (Such a funny joke—the women nearly died laughing.) It's all starlit skies and gambolling puppies. In the town history book, his mother tells her story again, and, though the old girl never much liked her, she weeps for the narrowness of a life which only knew one story of its own—this small adventure of revived peafowl.

Long after they buy the tent, she keeps the faith. She keeps the faith even when he says if something should happen to him, it would be unnatural of her to take up with another man, unnatural of her to bear another's man child but the same would not be true in reverse. She keeps the faith even when he tells her (shaking his head ruefully) that, once raped, a woman is no good, no longer desirable, and throughout his lessons in animal husbandry: father over daughter is acceptable, but never mother over son. She believes in him enough to confess the reason she cries during sex—he never minds this—and when he screws up his face, she blames herself for his distaste.

Somewhere in the high plains—might have been Dargo, might have been Bogong—her nightmare cries become tedious. He tells her she is claustrophobic in the tent and she believes him.

And when he calls her disturbed, she believes that too.

They're at a club dinner, he in the intricate Aran sweater she knitted for him with all its complex diamonds and cables, she in the black evening dress that makes her feel, if not sophisticated, then at least like she might become so one day, when he notices another girl at their table and sits up straight. He lights the other girl's cigarette before lighting his own. Removing the cigarette from between her lips, she lays it on the table.

Outside, she appeals to the moon with foggy eyes. It has been one of those balmy spring days one can never quite believe will turn chill at night, but it is chill now, brutally so. Experience has taught her that frost is the price of clear skies and brilliant stars. Gazing upon the night vista shared with him these past years, she acknowledges how she merely inhabits a girl-shaped vacancy in his life, like a promising jigsaw puzzle piece which disappoints once pressed to the picture. She is not sunshine enough.

Time will obscure her last visit to the farm, why she went, whether she stopped at the end of the driveway to clear her eyes before taking to the road. She tries to remember the journey home but cannot, only that once there, she sat in a patch of fading sun on the living room floor listening to music and drinking too much. But it is just for today. Just today. That was the start of it.

She will recall it was still spring the last time she saw him, a spring day riotously indifferent to her impending winter, and how, as she was leaving, he delayed her with an urgent gesture to ask, what do you want to do about the tent? And she had never known him to reach for his wallet with such alacrity.

The Bloodwood Motel

Julie Fison

Alice's first thought is bloodied body parts. Maybe it's the disturbing state of the motel room, maybe it's the number of Crime shows she's watched lately, for some reason her mind conjures up severed limbs as she looks at the nylon sports bag, wedged behind the blankets on the top shelf of the wardrobe. She sniffs the air, assuming a bundle of rotting flesh would have a distinctive smell, but it's the stale, musty smell of disuse that dominates the room. She drops the blankets to the floor, disturbing more dust mites and a gecko, that runs for cover and disappears behind the bag. Alice edges closer. Still nothing to suggest death.

'What exactly are you up to?' Nadine croaks from the single bed in the corner. Five hours of eighties anthems on the road from home have clearly taken a toll on her vocal cords. Following the *Communards* into the falsetto register was never going to end well.

'There's a bag at the back of the wardrobe,' Alice says. 'Just a bit worried what might be in it.'

Nadine gets to her feet and inspects the contents of the bar fridge. There's a bottle of champagne that Alice put in there ten minutes earlier, two lonely cans of beer and a cluster of jam packets.

'Some of these have definitely been opened,' Nadine says, holding up a tiny packet of apricot conserve.

'What about the bag?' Alice says. 'What do you think's in it?'

'Could be a bomb.'

'A bomb?' Alice repeats. She lived in London in the nineties when the IRA's campaign to kick Britain out of Northern Ireland gave everyone reason to treat all abandoned packages like lethal devices, but Alice hadn't even considered a bomb. Until now. 'Who'd want to blow up the Bloodwood Motel?'

'Someone offended by the low standards of hygiene.'

Alice glances around the room, her eyes reluctantly settling on a polyester bedspread. 'I haven't seen geometric prints like that since Duran Duran ruled the charts.'

'Just don't look too closely at the sink. There's a pile of whiskers wedged behind the tap.'

'Oh my God. Now I've got a visual I won't be able to unsee. I just hope Donna doesn't notice. You think I should warn her?'

Nadine says no, but Alice knocks on the bathroom door anyway, calling to her friend. The shower is thundering into the dinky little tray, drowning out her voice, so there's no reply. Alice steps away from the bathroom, which isn't easy in such a confined space and ends up in front of the wardrobe, staring at the bag again. 'I'm calling reception.' She picks up the avocado-green handset on the bedside table, and presses the button for reception. There's a tinny dial tone, but no one answers. She remembers the bloke at the front desk taking their details on a post-it note because the computer was *playing silly buggers* and mentioning something about bingo. He's probably already gone.

'You getting room service?' Donna is standing at the bathroom door, her hair wet from the shower, a sequined Camilla hanging loosely from her shoulders. The vibrant kaleidoscope of leopard print, protea and cockatoos adding a possibly unprecedented amount of glamour to the dingy room. Donna is not the sort to let her surroundings dictate her sartorial choices. 'A Bellini and a dozen oysters for me.'

'Of course, madam,' Alice says with an obsequious nod of her head. 'The lobster to follow?'

'Well why the hell not? It's my birthday.' Donna laughs, her brown eyes twinkling for a moment, then her face drops. She slumps onto the nearest bed. 'Fifty sucks.'

Donna is taking the big Five-O thing very hard: the last of her kids heading off to uni in Melbourne, her husband disappearing into the sunset, with a glamorous Argentinian woman with a passion for polo and younger men, after draining the cash from her business, have all definitely put a dampener on the milestone. But Alice is determined to see her enjoy the occasion.

'Fifty is the new thirty!' she says, even though Alice knows fifty is the start of a long list of complaints: knee pain, hip issues, weight gain, not to mention night sweats, plus a bowel cancer test kit that turns up unsolicited in the mail. Hardly the ideal birthday gift.

'That's just marketing bullshit.' Nadine chimes in, totally eroding Alice's attempt to elevate Donna's spirits.

'*Quintastic*—it's a thing.' Alice presses on. She pulls out her phone, looking for evidence, but the internet is on a go-slow strike. She watches the blue line crawl at glacial pace across the search window. 'Here we go,' Alice says eventually. She skims over a story about fifty being the age that women become invisible, eventually opening a piece on Jennifer Lopez hitting her half century and still looking red hot in fishnets and some kind of bustier. *Maybe not*. Alice comes up with a story about fifty real women doing extraordinary things in their fifties, but by then Donna has totally lost interest in being Quintastic and has noticed the black bag.

'What's that?'

'Possibly a bomb,' Nadine reports. 'Or maybe some itinerant worker topped himself in here and left his clothes behind.'

Alice glares at Nadine, trying to discourage her speculation, but Donna seems excited. She gets to her feet, peers into the wardrobe. '*Oh, I get it.*' A conspiratorial smile spreads across her face as she glances from Nadine to Alice. '*You girls* ... I told you *no presents*. Just having you here ... it's more than enough.'

Nadine frowns. 'That's good. Because it's all you've got. A long weekend in the middle of no fucking where and us. Livin' the dream, babe!' The sounds of the street drift in through the barred open window. Cicadas humming, a mopoke calling to its mate and someone chucking on the footpath even though it's barely six.

'We should have gone to Byron,' Alice mumbles.

Donna doesn't seem to register the comment. Her eyes are fixed on the bag, like she's sizing up what kind of lovely surprise might be inside. She yanks it off the top shelf. It falls to the threadbare carpet with a heavy thump, mould spores flying into the air.

'Donna, it's not a birthday present,' Alice says. 'But it's two-for-one night at the bistro across the road and the bar's doing Karaoke later. What more could you want?'

Donna hoiks up her dress and drops to the floor, takes hold of the bag's zip, yanks so hard, the slider comes off in her hand. '*Oh, crap.*' She holds it out, as if Alice might be able to offer some solution to the problem.

Alice shakes her head, helplessly. She wonders if it's too late to nip out and buy a little gift. Even a Mills and Boon and a packet of Tim Tams from the funny little shop on the main street might be enough to save the evening.

Nadine, ever the Girl Guide, hands Donna a Swiss army knife.

What is she hoping to achieve? The bag can't possibly contain anything that's going to lift Donna's spirits, unless someone's left a chilled bottle of Louis Roederer and a pair of diamond studs inside. That's even less likely than a bomb. And then Alice starts to worry that it really could be a bomb. 'You sure you should be opening that?'

Donna flicks out the blade, holds the knife high and then plunges it into the thin black nylon. Logically Alice knows it's not a bomb, but her instinct for self-preservation gets the better of her and she grabs a pillow from the nearest bed, drops to the floor, the thundering in her chest almost matching the labouring bar fridge.

The hacking finally stops.

'You have got to be fucking kidding me!' Nadine shouts.

Alice peaks over the top of the extra-firm Tontine. *What the hell.* It's not a bomb, or body parts, or an itinerant's discarded clothes, it's cash tumbling onto the floor. Piles and piles of it, covering the brown carpet. She grabs the empty black bag, inspecting the outside, turning it inside out and assessing the lining, but there's no name, nothing to indicate who the bag belongs to or where it came from. It's just a plain black sports bag. Even the label is too faded to read. Alice picks up a one hundred dollar note, gazing at old Sir John Monash for answers, but his walrus moustache and battle-weary face give nothing away.

Nadine runs her hands through the notes, absently sorting the money into piles. Her auditing days long behind her, but her fingers apparently haven't forgotten what's required. 'It's thousands. Might even be ... a hundred thousand bucks.'

Donna gets to her feet, clutching a bundle of fifties. 'I knew the universe would provide.' She drifts across the room, her long silk dress catching a few notes on the way past. A trail of blue and red bills follow her to the window. She fans herself with the fifties, gazing outside, a million miles away.

Nadine retrieves a ten dollar note from under Donna's dress, restores it to the proper place. 'You know we have to take it to the police. We have to do the right thing.'

Donna stares at the motel forecourt a little longer, then turns with a defeated sigh, drops her bundle of fifties into the wrong pile. 'Where has that ever got anyone.' She trudges to her suitcase, pulls out a tropical print purse and removes a lipstick. Using the mottled surface of the kettle, she applies a soft pink, tears welling in her eyes.

'C'mon,' Alice says. 'You're a kick ass entrepreneur, a great mother and you're hot as hell. You'll get things back on track. And we're all here for you.' She says it with genuine sincerity but something about the dilapidated state of the room makes her words sound hollow. She really wishes she'd overruled Nadine and booked a beachfront apartment for Donna's birthday. She pulls the champagne from the bar fridge, wondering if a tepid drink might improve Donna's mood. She's looking for glasses when something catches her eye. A tiny purple tablet is caught in the folds of the patterned bedspread. She bends down, takes a closer look, picking up the pill and turning it over in her hand. Her guts tighten as she assesses the unmistakable crown stamp. *'Ecstasy,'* Alice whispers without hesitation. Her daughter ended up in hospital on life support after taking a contaminated pill at a music festival last year. Nadine's daughter in the ward down the hall, almost as close to death. A sickening feeling rises into her throat as she remembers the call from the hospital, the mad dash down the highway, the hours in the waiting room, not knowing if her daughter would pull through.

Donna gives the bedspread a shake. Another two colourful pills fall to the floor. 'It's got to be drug money, right? The owner's probably in jail. No point taking it to the police.'

'If we keep the money, it makes us criminals, too,' Alice says. But even as she's saying it, she's peeling a fifty from the top of the bag. She takes another. Then another. Ending up with a handful of money. Holding the cash, she waits for the guilt to creep up her spine, but the only disturbance comes from her rumbling stomach. It's hours since they stopped for lunch—a cafe in Chinchilla that served salad sandwiches the old way—with shredded carrot and slices of tinned beetroot, on soft white bread. Her stomach rumbles again. Alice glances from Nadine to Donna, sucks in a long breath, then puts the cash in her pocket. The sports bag goes under the bed. She grabs the room key.

'I think we should get over to the pub and order dinner before the kitchen closes. We've got a fiftieth to celebrate.'

Escape From Execution

Sagamba Muhira and James Page

There were many times during the Congo Wars when ordinary people would narrowly escape death. One weekday stands out in my memory. I was only young at the time, but I can remember the key events of this day in detail. I was travelling back from Goma, heading for my home town of Sake, after having finished school for the week. I had just started secondary school in Goma, only twenty-five kilometres from my home.

On that afternoon I was riding with five fellow students in the back of a pick-up truck, heading back to Sake. I cannot recall, at that stage, talking to those with me in the pick-up. We just stared out at the passing countryside, as we drove along the road. This was a sealed road, and thus the driver was able to drive quite fast. As the pick-up sped over the crests in the road, we would momentarily become air-borne, and then come back down on our seats. On corners and curves, we indeed were hanging on tight, as the driver warned us. Although it was a hot day, the speed of the truck meant that the rush of the air cooled us down. It was gently hilled country—pastureland, with very few trees, as most of the these had been long ago cut down for firewood. But I was feeling good.

We passed by an area which we knew had been the location of a large refugee encampment on the side of the road. We also knew it was likely there would be soldiers nearby. As we came around a slight corner, we saw a tree across the road, with a large 'STOP' sign nearby. This probably had been a traffic sign in Goma, which had been stolen for the purpose of signalling the road-block. There was also a soldier with an AK-47 assault rifle, gesturing for us to stop. It was the mid-afternoon, about 3pm. Three other soldiers soon joined him. It was common for soldiers to set up roadblocks as a means of raising money. It had been a clear sunny day, and I remember that the sun was still high and hot in the western sky.

I remember that the rifles of the soldiers were not merely slung over their backs. They were holding them at the ready, with fingers on the triggers.

One soldier walked up to the pick-up. He looked at those in the back of the pick-up and then pointed at three of us. He gestured towards the ground and called out: 'Get down!' In circumstances like this it is best to comply with instructions, so I jumped down from the pick-up. At no time did the soldier ask what my ethnic group was, although from his actions it was quite obvious that he had made an identification based upon our ethnic appearance.

'Show us your ID,' was the soldier's next command. I complied, showing him my student card. He looked briefly at the card—I think he wasn't really interested in this, but rather just wanted to see if I had any ID at all. Initially I was told to sit down at the side of the road. He just pointed to a place beside the pick-up truck and said. 'Sit there!' At that stage, he waved to the driver of the pick-up to drive away, which he did. This worried me. It meant there were no witnesses to what might happen.

There were two other guys from my ethnic group, older teenagers and fellow students from the Masisi region, and they too were ordered to sit by the side of the road. After about five minutes, the soldiers told us to move to another area, about 100 metres away from the road. I was very afraid, especially as this area was further from public view, but said absolutely nothing, and continued to do as I was told. We walked to the new area, with soldiers on each side of us, all with guns pointing at us.

I did briefly think of making a run for it, but my heart said: 'These guys will shoot if we try anything.' Besides, there was the problem that all the trees had been cut down, and thus there was nowhere to run to. In the Congo, we believe that everyone has a time to die. So, I thought, let's find out if today is that day. At that time, I didn't think that there would be killing. I thought that at the most we would get a beating.

Once in this new holding area, we were told to remove our shirts and shoes, and we placed these neatly in a pile. The three of us were sitting down, with our arms around our knees, and not making any eye contact with the soldiers. You don't make eye contact in situations like this, because those with the guns will think that you are challenging them. You just look straight ahead of you, or at the ground. And because we were in the midst of so many troops, the soldiers nearby no longer pointed their weapons at us. There was no possibility of escape, so no-one needed to point their weapons at us.

Soon the soldiers starting yelling and swearing at us. And asking us questions, like: 'Who do you work with? Where do you come from? Who is your father? Who is your mother? Why don't you go back to Rwanda?' If any of us didn't answer promptly, then we were prompted to answer by the jab of a rifle butt to the body. When talking with each other, the soldiers would refer to us as 'these stupid people,' and other expressions that I don't want to repeat here.

After a time, they started a new form of interrogation. A soldier would walk up to us, and stand on our toes whilst asking a question. I cried out in pain. But the two older guys didn't say anything. I think they wanted not to show fear, and to show they were not intimidated. That may have been a mistake. The troops with the guns said, 'You didn't cry out just now. This proves that you are enemy soldiers, as only a person with military training would know not to cry out.' It was a nonsense conclusion, but logic didn't play a great role in what was happening.

Then something fortunate happened for me. A soldier, not part of the initial process, then joined in. This soldier looked at me, and he paused a little. He then called out to me: 'Hey, your face is familiar. Where are you from? Aren't you the son of Muhira?' That was the break that would save my life.

'Yes, that's me. I'm his eldest son.'

'Oh, yeah. Hey, your dad is a good man, I know him well.'

From that point onwards, the soldiers started to leave me alone. But I was still sitting down, leaning forward with my hands around my knees.

A few moments later, an officer came over to where we were sitting. Unlike the other soldiers, he was clean shaven and well-dressed. He pointed to the two teenagers, and said: 'Hey, you two, you're filthy; you need to wash yourselves. This soldier will take you to the shower over there, where you can clean yourselves up.'

It was an order which didn't quite make sense, but in circumstances like this, you don't argue. The boys silently followed the soldier to the tap, about 50 metres away. The tap was at chest level, and above this was a plank, with two soldiers standing on the plank, running next to the tap. Both the soldiers were holding axe handles.

It was an ominous situation, but the two teenagers had few options. The two turned on the tap, bent over, and started washing themselves, as they had been told. Without any warning, the two soldiers lifted their axe-handles, and started clubbing and smashing the heads of the two teenagers. The attack was so sudden that the two had no chance to run for safety, and were dead within a few minutes. Even though this was only about fifty metres from me, it was terrible to see, and terrible to hear. I will never forget the sight of what I saw, the sounds, and the screams.

The location of the killing was very convenient, as water from the tap was used to clean up the resulting mess. The officer's wishes were fulfilled. Everything was clean.

I don't know what happened to the bodies. I was too scared and shocked at what I had experienced to really take it all in. I assume that the bodies were dumped in a nearby river. In the Congo, there are bodies everywhere.

After I saw what had happened to the two teenagers, I put my head back down on my knees. I was too scared to watch any more. Eventually the commander arranged for some soldiers to drive me back to my home in Sake. I could not believe what I had witnessed. When I came back home I was shaking and crying. For many days I couldn't sleep. And now, many years later, I still sometimes have nightmares about what happened on that day.

Sadly, for the parents of the two teenage boys, and for many others in the Congo, this was just part of what was happening daily in the Congo. The two young boys had been killed merely because they were from the Masisi district, and they were perceived to be of military age by virtue of their ethnic group they were perceived to be a potential enemy. This is the nature of ethnic war. The only reason that I was spared was through a family connection.

For the families of the two boys, the worst part of the killing is that they would never know what happened to their young sons. All that they would know is that one day two boys simply never returned home from a visit to Goma. There would be no opportunity to grieve their loss and to give their sons a proper burial, something which is very important in African culture. I never knew the names of the two Masisi teenagers, but on that day they became two of the many millions of people who disappeared during the Congo Wars.

Sometimes, talking about this event makes me feel bad. But it is sometimes good to talk about things you feel bad about in your heart because unless you do talk about these things, then the bad things stay in your heart. It is hard to build a future on the past, when the past is bad. But it is important to recognise the bad things of the past. Later, in the years after this event, I came to learn that many people in the Congo had experienced terrible things, and it is important to share. People were killed everywhere, but sharing gives you the opportunity to help other people who have also experienced terrible things, and perhaps together we can help ensure such events never happen again.

The Great Easter Let Down

Todd Alexander

I wanted to get out of there more than I wanted anything else in the world. If our suburb was a jigsaw puzzle of same-same houses on hot, non-descript streets then I was that piece near the corner which didn't quite fit. Never mind, put me in my place and bash me down with your fist and it might just look as though I belonged there like everyone else. Most nights I'd lay awake staring at the ceiling, imagining what life could be like somewhere else. I invented ways of escape, would bargain chunks of my soul, my brain, selected body parts—anything to be free of the straight jacket I was forced to wear every day.

Hi God, this is Todd. If I give you the little finger on my left hand would you consider ... Hi Satan, this is Todd. You can take my intelligence if you just ...

I wasn't fussy—anyone who'd come to my rescue could have just about anything they liked.

When Mum and Dad sat us down to have one of 'those' chats in early 1989, I secretly hoped it was to tell us they were getting a divorce. I thought being a child of divorce would make me more edgy, more interesting. A small part of me wanted to get lost in the drama of it all. There would be the division of their possessions and sons, us choosing who we'd prefer to live with. Grant, the eldest, would undoubtedly choose Dad so they could get lost in a world of sport, Glen and I would, of course, choose Mum. Glen was the self-elected President of the AGA (Anti-Grant Association), and had recently taken to waving placards calling for the EPFG (Equal Punishment for Grant). Without having much say in the matter, I'd also been recruited. It just seemed Grant could get away with murder whereas Glen and I were punished for the slightest offence.

Like the time Mum left us inside a parked car one night while she went to place some bets at the TAB. Unlike my father whenever he went to that land of promised riches, dressed in bum-crack revealing, too-tight shorts, a singlet and bare feet, at least my mother was wearing something more appropriate—a shoulder-padded knitted jumper that complemented the colour of her latest perm. Maybe Mum *would* copy Dad and whip her own arse with a rolled up form guide while screaming 'Ssss! Ssss!' at a horse on the telly

Suddenly, my bored brother decided to start using the dashboard and hazard lights to parade our Sydney Silkie Terrier, Lindy, around the car as the newly crowned Queen Lindy LuLuBelle of Lindyland. Glen was forever inventing things for us to pass the time. It's as if he had this evil voice inside his head regularly whispering: 'why don't you do something really stupid to royally piss off your mother? And, while you're at it, why don't you drag your little brother into it too?'

Partway through the doggy parade, we noticed a man sitting in the car next to us. He was bald, evil-eyed and staring at us like a child-molester not long escaped from Long Bay. Well, that's how Glen described him. Doors locked, we bobbed down on the floor in the back and occasionally peeked up to see him still staring.

After an eternity of near-abduction tension, Mum finally returned from the TAB and, when she put the car in reverse, Glen and I grinned satisfyingly at the man and gave him a curt little wave.

In a flash of astonishing cinematic swiftness, the man flew up out of his seat, floated out of his car, and was instantaneously behind our Bluebird 180B. He was bashing the boot for Mum to stop. We came to a sudden halt, then the dangerous criminal was tapping at the glass next to her face.

'Don't—' Glen said with a gulp, but it was too late. Mum was winding down her window. Now all three of us would perish. It was all Glen's fault.

'Your kids ...' the man said. 'They scared the life out of me. I thought your car was on fire! It was all orange! They were screaming and carrying on, I didn't know what to do!'

'Thank you,' my mother said calmly. She wound her window up and continued reversing. The silence suffocating the ten-minute drive home told us exactly what to expect.

Mum had one golden rule: *do not embarrass me*. We'd learnt that lesson when the Stewart family arrived at our doorstep for an un-announced visit once and Mum met them at the door where she basically stood her ground and refused to let them in. While she was doing her best to provide upbeat banter, my brothers and I were in the dining room window behind the Stewarts' backs making faces at Mum. As soon as they left she went to the hallway cupboard, retrieved her pink feather-duster and asked us to stand still while she whipped our legs with the cane.

When we got home from the TAB that night, the same feather-duster fate fell upon Glen and me and while the crack of the cane no longer made us cry (unless we got our knuckles in the way) it still smarted enough for you to dread it like a fat kid dreads taking his top off for swimming lessons.

But had Grant been the one 'bunging it on' outside the TAB, he either would've outrun his punisher or talked her down from the ledge, so this was why the AGA had been forced to ramp up its activities.

While the divorce lines had more or less already been drawn by us kids (even despite Mum's occasional whipping of our legs), that wasn't what our parents wanted to talk about that night in early 1989.

Dad had been offered a new job (so far, so good), a great job in an exciting company (excellent), in fact, he'd been poached by the business owner (*well how 'bout that? Nice one, Dad*) ... but the company was on the Central Coast ... a three hour drive away and so, just like that, within a couple of months the entire family would be moving. It hardly seemed fair. Surely Dad could just do the three-hour commute each way and leave us all the hell alone, exactly where we were.

At this time we were living in the newish housing estate called St Clair, where we'd been for about eight years. Almost every day of my teenage life, I'd longed to get out of there, looked for ways to escape, trying different scenarios on to test their fit. One had always been divorce. Mum would choose to take Glen and me to a different place, a better place, where miraculously I'd be allowed to be me without any sense of shame. Another was Mum and Dad winning the lottery and the time Mum won twelve hundred bucks had been altogether thrilling ... but wasn't quite enough to buy us a mansion overlooking the harbour. When the fantasies all boiled down, whenever I concentrated on my future, I realised my brain was my ticket out of St Clair and, in only a few years, I would run away from it and never come back. I was going to University and from my very first day in that very first lecture, everything would instantly feel safer ... better.

'When are we moving?' Grant asked. My mind was reeling but I could still detect the uncertainty in his voice. It would take me decades to work out just how similar he and I often are.

'We need to choose a house first,' Mum said all excitedly.

'It's gonna be so great for all of us.' Dad was beaming.

'But I work in Seven Hills ...' Grant pressed on. He was working as a teller in a branch at the back of an industrial estate. The Central Coast to Seven Hills was one hell of a commute for a guy who'd had the same best friend since the first day of kindergarten and had dreams of living in our same suburb for the term of his natural life.

'I'll drive you to work every day,' Mum said. She worked in Rydalmere not far from Grant's bank.

Glen was already gone. In a precursor for what was to become of his life, he'd applied to become a Rotary Exchange Student and was partway through his year abroad in New York.

Right away, I could tell Grant was resigned to the move. It just wasn't in his nature to protest against anything Mum and Dad decided was best for the family. Mum looked so happy with the news and Dad was proud of what this meant for the family. Where was Glen when I needed him? Where were the placards? The Anti-Moving Association could be born. Like Glen had done with his Western Suburbs black and white, I'd wave flags on the front lawn too—*beep if you don't want the Alexanders to move!*

'I don't want to change schools ...' I said barely above a whisper.

'We can get you into one of the best schools, Skeet,' Dad said. He didn't use my nickname (Amos-Quito) often, so I knew it was meant to soften the blow.

A radical idea popped into my brain. 'If Mum is driving Grant to Seven Hills, I could just get the train from there to school ...'

As much as I felt desperate to get out of St Clair like Glen had, we'd been on holidays to the Central Coast often enough for me to know that it was positively the furthest thing from the escape I craved. If I hated St Clair, the Coast was the equivalent of water torture. All I knew of it, from our sandy and sunburnt holidays, was shirtless, barefoot boys my age, girls hanging off their arms, firm muscular bodies, long surf-bleached hair, surfboards tucked beneath their arms and always this supreme sense of invincibility—that their hometown would never be welcoming to an outsider like me, particularly one from the West. I was untanned, overweight, had zero athleticism, lacked confidence, and possessed a boofy head of thick fluffy hair.

Praying had become an autopilot practice for me. I was Catholic and knew the words to 'The Lord's Prayer' and 'Hail Mary' and said them every night before sleep, never once noting the meaning. Then of course there was the real thigh-slapper, 'Gentle Jesus' which told kids it was a possibility they could die in their sleep. Some nights, I'd wake and sit bolt upright in bed, suddenly remembering that I'd forgotten to say my prayers, knowing how this put me in imminent danger of God taking me. In a semi-awake state, I'd run through the words of the prayers in my head and only once complete could I then (safely) drift off to sleep.

But not that night. That night, I said every word with emphasis, noted the meaning of every line, and at the end of my prayers I added something a little special: *please God, we both know last time I asked you for something like this, you really let me down. When I was ten, I prayed and prayed and begged you to let it be me who won that giant Easter egg at the school's Easter Parade raffle and you didn't, did you? But this time it's different—now you really have a chance to prove to me that you exist. Please help me God and I swear I will never ask for another thing. Please don't make us move. Don't let this happen to me.*

Beyond Patchy

Andrea Campbell

'How long to Hildy's place?' said the Boy.

'I reckon about an hour, as the crow flies.'

The man felt the Boy's hazel eyes on him. The Boy had his mother's eyes, the sort that could see right through you, clear and bold.

Their car was sending the Mallee dust flying. No matter what, they couldn't escape the dust. There it sat, as far as the horizon, a powdery brown stain against the blue sky.

The man jerked his chin at the windscreen. 'Hey look, what's that up there?' he said.

'An eagle. King of the land and the sky.'

The Boy was smiling with satisfaction.

The man scratched his head. He was almost out of diversions. It had been a long trip, and come hell or high water, they must get to Hildy's. They'd used up the fruit-picking money, and his pension wasn't due until next week. That welfare woman had been good, handing out fuel vouchers, but things were very tight. The worst moments were in the shops, where you'd have tins of food and soap and a tube of toothpaste and hope that they'd make it through. Most times, you were bailed-up at the end, and you had to choose what needed to go back. He'd hold onto the food, and let the rest go.

Lucky that he had his little system in place. When he was too broke to get everything he wanted at one place, he'd drive to the next town, and buy one or two items at the usual shop that sold hot food and doubled as a supermarket. He'd stand casually at the checkout, his arms resting against his jacket, feeling the items poking into his ribs that he'd lifted off the shelves. Although he wouldn't go so far as to believe in guardian angels, he had an idea that something was keeping an eye out for him in these moments. He knew he'd been seen slipping packets of lollies and shaving gear inside his jacket, but somehow, nothing ever happened. He always left the shop a free man.

'Grandad, when we get to Hildy's, I'm not going back to school,' the Boy said.

'Come again?'

'Well, I've missed too much school and there's no point going back. I can look after Hildy's chickens. She paid me for it last time, so I'll do it again and then we'll have some money.'

'You're going back to school.'

He thought of the Boy, and how when they stayed with Hildy, he'd taken the broody hens to bed with him. Funny little bugger. He was like his mother, a real softie for animals. He hoped that he'd only got all the good things from her, like his massive dark eyes and love of living things. Straying into the past, the man's mind dredged up sludgy memories. He thought of the drugs, those bloody things that killed the Boy's mother, and with the little fella sleeping beside her in his cot. Thank God the Boy was too young to remember.

So far, this part of the trip had gone without a hitch, but you never know. The man's eyes scanned the flat landscape for threats. The cops would have a field day with the near-bald tyres and chipped windscreen of his ute. He sighed at how run-down she was. She'd been a truly great old lady, always giving from her inexhaustible heart, offering them a bed under the stars and getting them places when all she could do was limp.

'Are you sure you're okay now, Grandad?' said the Boy. 'You looked really crook in hospital, with all those tubes going into your arm.'

The man's lips curled upwards.

'Of course I'm fine,' he said. 'I wouldn't be here with you, would I, driving you to Hildy's if I was sick. You've got nothing to worry about.'

He felt the Boy's eyes pass over him slowly, judging him for every cell in his body, seeing if he could really pass muster. That was why they had to get to Hildy's. He'd had the lump taken out, and then they'd given him stuff that made him even sicker. Now that he'd come good for a spell, he was doing what he could to tidy things up for the Boy. Hildy would step into the breach, if the worst happened. She'd always been the strong one, even when the drought had milked her land dry beyond recognition. Hildy was rock solid. There were few like her.

He swore under his breath. Now it was looking as though their luck was running out. They'd hardly passed any cars on this stretch of road, but there were two pulled up, not far away. This with the flashing blue light of a police car. Just stay calm, calm does it. He braked at the command to stop.

'Where are you off to?' The man in uniform had an affable, round face.

'Other side of Patchewollock.'

'Patchy, aye? What's going on there?'

'Seeing my sister.'

The cop looked away, up the road. 'Know another route to Patchy?' he said.

'I reckon I do,' said the man.

The cop was smiling a bent sort of smile.

'Well then, I reckon you'd better use it. We've got a truck up the road that's dropped all its stuff. Take some time to re-load. Wouldn't want you two to get held up, seeing you have important family business to attend to.'

'Sure thing.'

This meant that the sun was low in the sky when Hildy's old house swung into view. He roused the Boy from sleep.

'Wake up, we're here.'

The Boy jumped as though electrically charged.

They made their way cautiously through the screen door, avoiding contact with the bulging and broken wire.

'Fine time to arrive. You were meant to be here days ago.'

There was Hildy, clean apron on, rolling pin under one arm, and a wooden spoon in her hand. She waved the spoon at them.

'So sorry, old girl,' he said, and he tottered slowly towards her, and kissed her cheek. 'Would have got in touch, but that mobile phone thing in my pocket has died. You know, you can't put coins in them to keep them going.'

'Batch of scones on the table, not long out of the oven,' said Hildy to the Boy.

With the ice broken, the man wandered out back, and surveyed the sagging chicken coops and rusty water tanks. A tractor with a flat tyre was parked by the big shed. He clicked his tongue.

'Okay for you to come here and tut-tut.' Hildy was right behind him. He hadn't heard her coming.

'Here, this has been waiting for you a good two weeks.' She handed him a long white envelope, the sort with the name of a hospital on one corner.

Sitting on a crushed petrol drum, he ripped at the envelope with a dirty fingernail. He fumbled with the contents, his massive dusty thumbprints peppering the paper. His head fell to his knees. It was as if the bones had been sucked from his body, and he'd been put through a huge mincing machine and turned to a pasty jelly.

'You okay?'

Hildy's voice sounded compressed, as though she were speaking from the bottom of the sea. He lifted his eyes to face her apron, swollen as it was with the contours of her generous stomach.

'Here, have a look at this, Hild,' he said. 'You'd make more damn sense of this than I can.'

She grabbed the paper from him.

'Well,' she said. 'It's certainly got a lot to say.'

She saw the deep lines criss-crossing his face, and sensed his residual pain. He looked as if something were eating him, tearing into his head and eyes, like the carcass of an animal by the roadside when the crows started on it.

'What do you reckon?' he said.

'Know what I reckon?' she said. 'I reckon you're going to be all right. There's words here in this letter … something about "clear" and "no sign". Yes, I think it's saying that you'll do. You're still going to be on this earth to plague me.'

They looked at each other in disbelief, their eyes teary. They staggered in unison, and the staggering became a drunken dance, their hands resting on their shoulders, their footfalls clomping and heavy. With every step, they seemed to be sinking further and further into the dust. They didn't hear the Boy until he jumped in between them, shouting.

'What's going on?' the Boy said.

'We're going on,' said Hildy. 'We're getting you back to school, and your Grandad's going to get the tractor started again, and build me a new roof.'

The Boy scowled. 'What's so good about that?' he said. 'School's pretty useless.'

'There's lots of roast dinners in it for you. Get that brain of yours trained up like an Olympic athlete,' said Hildy, and she turned on her heels and scuttled off to the kitchen, leaving the man and the Boy with the chickens that pecked at their feed in the dusk.

Anyone Home?

Jennifer Hand

I'm standing beside the window. I do it sometimes. There's a sliver of view of the garden through the space where the blind doesn't touch the window frame. I can see the sun on the grass and the black shadow of the hedge slanting across the drive. Sometimes I catch a glimpse of someone passing by the end of the hedge just as it leans over the drive. Sometimes, I see a woman staring up the drive, looking puzzled and curious. No one can see me though. I am pressed close to the wall.

I think I'm feeling OK today. I think I can do it. I slide my hand between the blind and the window frame and open up the view a bit more. I can see most of the drive now. I can see where Carol's car used to be. She was very proud when she got it. She came racing in; one huge smile.

'Look, Mum, I bought it. What do you think? Do you love it?'

'I love it,' Mum said. 'Well done, you! You must be proud. I'm so proud of you.'

'Come for a ride in it, Mum,' Carol pleaded. 'Go on! Let me take you for a drive.'

Mum's face lit up for a moment.

'I'd love it,' she said. Then she looked at me, her face closing down.

'You come, Robbie,' she said.

My head started to shake on my neck and my whole body was trembling. Carol's shiny look went dulled too.

'Can't we leave him Mum? Just 'round the block? Two minutes.' She looked at me, her mouth set.

'Or you could come. You'll be in the car. You'll be safe.'

I shook my head. I couldn't help it: shaking. Mum came over to me. She put her arm around my shoulders and ruffled my hair.

'He can't help it, Carol.' Her voice was soft and low. She wanted Carol to understand. Carol should understand. I can't help it. So I come first.

The car's not there now. Carol sold it before she left.

While I've been remembering, that woman's come past. She's staring up the drive again. I've still got my hand between the blind and the window. I stare back for a second. Sometimes I do this. I'm sure people can't see me here, pressed up against the wall, but I'm starting to stress. I let go quickly. I'm still shaking.

Carol made me go for treatment after Mum died. The psychiatrist said I wasn't too bad. He said that Carol could look after me. That I could have treatment and I could be an outpatient. He said someone could come to our house and talk to me about my condition and help me. He said I should challenge myself a bit. A little at a time, he said.

After that I tried going out at night. I'd go out on dark nights, when there was no moon. Or when there were lots of clouds or even rain. I would go into the front garden. I would walk across the lawn down to the hedge. It wasn't so big and thick then and I could see through it. There aren't any people around in the middle of the night. I would imagine walking over to the drive and going through the gate onto the footpath. I will be able to do it soon, I thought. I'm building up to it, I thought. I still trembled and my head and my hands still shook but I wasn't so fearful. Adrenalin rush. I'd read about it on the net. Some people like it, they said. Especially teenage boys and young men. They called it excitement, not fear. I will like it, I decided. One day I will like it.

I usually slipped away inside if I heard someone walking on the footpath. But one night, when I heard someone coming, I thought: this time I will like it. I will stay. I was trembling a bit; quite a lot, really. I tried to think I liked it but as they got closer I was shaking more and just as they reached the hedge my arms sort of shot out and started the hedge shaking. The person's head jerked round. They were wearing one of those torches on their head, a headlamp, and it shone straight in my eyes. I held my breath but they must have seen my face peering through the hedge. I saw their eyes widen and they screamed. And I screamed back and I couldn't stop and I ran inside. Inside, I wobbled and jerked and fell into the black.

I didn't go out at all for a long time after that. I wouldn't see the person coming to treat me. Carol would just talk to her.

I don't know what the person said to Carol but after a bit Carol threatened to leave if I didn't try. I started going out into the back garden. I'd just go out for a bit and sit there with my eyes closed. I could hear rustling noises in the shrubs but it wasn't people. Possums are OK. I kept doing this for a while but Carol said it wasn't enough. She said:

'I'm going to leave. There's more to life. I have a life too. I'm going to travel. Go overseas and see the world. It's my life too.'

'Mum said you have to look after me.' I said.

I knew she wouldn't really go. She had told Mum that she would look after me. I come first. But I went along with it. She taught me how to do the banking and to order food and meals on the net. She showed me that Mum had left us quite a lot of money and that every week some more money would come in. I learned how to pay the bills.

'I've made everything electronic so you won't always need to go out. You can order food in and have it delivered if you have attacks. We'll use my password just for now,' Carol said. 'Before I leave I'll set up your bank account. OK?'

I said OK but I knew she wouldn't go. She was just day-dreaming, but I went along. I pretended that I was doing better. I stayed out for longer. I said that I walked around a bit and went into the front garden. Once, I said that I had gone onto the footpath for a little bit. But really I stayed in the back garden with my eyes closed. One time quite a while later, she said:

'You know, you could go shopping at the supermarket in the middle of the night. They're open all night these days. There wouldn't be many people there. You could give that a go. We could do that soon if you like. We could set a day.'

I could hardly breathe.

'I'm not ready yet.' My voice went all squeaky and strained. 'No I'm not ready.'

'Well, you need to try to be better soon because I have advertised my car for sale and when it's gone I'll book my tickets.'

I tried not to show how angry I was. I think she couldn't tell the difference between angry shaking and scared shaking.

'You'll be fine,' she said in a high, gentle voice. But I wasn't soothed.

Her car sold very quickly. Well, it had never been driven very far, I suppose.

'The money's in the bank now,' she said. 'Tomorrow, I'll go to a travel agent. I'm excited you know. I wish you could be excited for me. Maybe you could try to get better and we could travel together.'

My voice came out all rough and loud.

'How can I?' I shouted. 'You said you'd look after me. You promised. You lied to Mum. You liar, you liar,' I screamed.

I got a shock when she screamed back. My head shook. I wanted to put my hands over my ears but my arms were jerking everywhere. So I heard her.

'You're a liar. Yes, you're a liar. Do you think I don't know that you haven't tried to get better? That I didn't see you just sitting there in the back garden? Why didn't you ever see the person who came to treat you? It's my life too!' She had tears pouring down her face. 'My life, get it? It isn't second to yours!'

I wanted to stop her. I wanted to put my hand over her mouth. My whole body was jerking and shaking and shuddering and then I fell into the black. The next morning when I woke up I was in bed. For a moment I thought it was all normal. Then I remembered Carol screaming at me. I started to shake again and wondered how she had got me to bed. She must have tried very hard. She's not big like me. I called out to her. But there was no answer. I went looking for her. She must have left already, I thought. She must have left in a rush—all her things were still there. She must have just gone.

She's been gone for ages now. She never even changed the bank to me. But I know how to use hers so that's what I do. She never uses it.

I'm not better. Since that last night with Carol, I don't even go into the back garden. I tried to once but there's a mound of dirt that's somehow grown next to the shrubs. Carol must have made it. It frightens me, so I can't go there.

What I do is stand beside the window and look through the sliver of space between the blind and the frame. Sometimes, I slide my hand between the blind and the window frame and open up the view a bit more. Today I can see that woman standing staring up the drive and looking at the garden. She's the one I've seen before. I am starting to shake. She'd better not come into the garden.

She'd better go away.

Firstborn

India Rose Thomas

'Annie.' Jude's low voice cuts through the evening hush as he calls her. 'Dad's coming by.'

Wrapped in a blanket on the couch, Annie turns to him. She takes in his slim frame angled in the doorway, lit up in gold by the setting sun. He looks heaven sent, she thinks with affection, even in Blundstone boots with a worry crease between his eyes.

'Do you want to tell him about the baby tonight?' he asks her softly. Annie shakes her head emphatically.

'Ten weeks is still too early. I know it's unlikely but imagine if …' She trails off. 'It'd be too much after …'

'My mum, yeah,' Jude finishes slowly. Annie wants to reach out and squeeze his hand, see his shoulders relax but he's standing too far away.

The sunset is lazy tonight, the kind that drenches the sky in light for hours. Clouds drift over the sea as if coloured by a careless toddler. Shades of pink, apricot, gold. From here on the veranda, the view is all big sky and the wide curves of hills that cradle the horizon. The warm air is like a caress. Late February, on the cusp of autumn. Jude unfolds himself from the doorway to settle beside Annie heavily. He looks tired.

'Okay, we won't tell him yet.' He sighs and rests a hand on her stomach, thumb gently tracing the growing curve protectively. He presses a swift kiss to her shoulder.

'Jude?'

'Mmm?'

Annie goes to ask him if he's okay, if there's anything she can do, but—'Don't let him in if he's been drinking.' The words tumble out in a rush.

She tries to stay impassive but her voice betrays her. There's a twinge in her belly and she surreptitiously flattens a hand to her navel anxiously.

'He's been better lately.' Jude's face is tight. He goes back inside. Dishes clatter in the sink, over the hum and clunk of water in the old pipes. Annie can hear the floorboards creaking underfoot as Jude moves back and forth between the table and the kitchen. She imagines him turning the plates under the hot soapy water in the same unhurried, careful way that he does everything. Like he has all the time in the world. Clearing the wine bottle (only for him now) before his father gets here (out of sight out of mind), the lasagne tray, the cutlery. Flicking the tap open to a gush, his ring glinting wet silver under the warm lamplight.

God, she loves him.

A few wasps drone languidly around the apple trees and drift over to the veranda, stupefied by the sweetness of the ripening fruit. The evening is a slow dream. Sometimes Annie feels like she's floating away on this couch, lulled by the far off sound of the waves, the tang of eucalyptus in the air. This is all she needs in the world. Just Jude and her and the changing light on the sea.

Selfish, maybe. But now there's a baby to think about. Their little bump of joy, untouched by grief. And they hope, quietly in the hours together in the dark late at night, a reason for Dan to finally stop drinking.

There's been a fragile peace in these last months between Jude and his father and Annie yearns for it desperately. There's no way she'll bring up a child in the presence of an alcoholic. She knows what it's like. She's lived that.

Surrounded by cricket song and the sweet smell of the grass, she takes a deep breath and lets it out slow, but images still erupt behind her eyes. The bright smash of bottles on the ground under her small bare feet—an accident, her father pleads—him wild eyed and inconsolable by eleven am, mouth open and slack, the bitterness of her own fear, the dank odour of the house, rain pressing close at the windows.

Her stomach cramps again and she's jolted from her thoughts. A sharp pain this time. Annie doubles over wordlessly. Is this a normal symptom of pregnancy? The crickets are suddenly deafening and panic pulses in her ears. Should have read those maternity books that Jude put on her bedside table last month more thoroughly, should have Googled more, drunk more mint tea, done more yoga.

Again the pain comes.

Annie stands, tangled in the blanket as she fumbles with her thick leather belt, bracing for a bloom of deep red between her legs. In the bathroom, she crumbles onto the toilet seat. Please, please no. Her private fear. She's whispering under her breath to the bump, shoving her jeans down frantically.

The white of her underwear is so stark and clean it's almost shocking.

She curls over in relief. Her head feels hot against her hands. Her tongue stings and there's a coppery taste in her mouth. She flushes the toilet, runs water, rinses her mouth. The spit in the sink is tinged with blood. Pulse still hammering, she lingers to touch the dried lavender hanging in the window and recollect herself. If she stills herself and listens hard, the silvery whisper of the sea is just audible.

She emerges from the bathroom to the rich scent of coffee, the percolator gurgling to life on the stove. Dan's dog Lena winds round her legs and shoots frantically out the door into the orchard, all inquisitive nose and trotting paws amongst the fallen apples. Dan is there in the kitchen with Jude. He's a big man. Fills up the space, straight-backed with heavy boots covered in dust. He moves with the kind of ease common in men of that age, sureness in every line of their bearing. Never doubting how they will be received. Damn them, Annie thinks with bitter envy. There are so many things men don't need to worry about.

But she's being unfair. He's had his share of grief, it's there in the lines of his face. Sorrow has aged him and weighed down his shoulders. Off balance and flushed, she pulls her long hair back and resists the urge to cradle her belly. The kitchen is thick with tension. She feels like an interloper.

Dan nods to Annie and goes to speak, lifting up one of his amber home brew bottles from beside his chair. Her stomach drops. She looks toward Jude, who is crossing the room holding three mugs of coffee.

His face darkens. He speaks roughly.

'Fuck, Dad! We made it clear that in this house—'

Dan cuts him off. He shakes his head frantically, entreating them to listen.

'I've stopped drinking.' He gestures to the tall bottle beside him and speaks quickly.

'It's the ginger beer I've been fermenting for Annie. I haven't had a drink for four weeks.' In his craggy face, his blue eyes, (so like Jude's) are bright and clear, his gaze steady.

'Wanted to make sure I could make a month sober before I told you.' There's a slight tremble in his voice and he moves to take a hurried sip of coffee.

Jude exhales in one slow breath, his face bright with emotion as he looks at his father. Hope has been something so delicate for so long. The relief feels like sinking into a warm bath. Jude's eyes flick to meet Annie's for a long heartbeat and she wants to soak up this moment for a little longer. Hidden from view by the table, she strokes the bump. The velvety night has fallen outside the windows. In the stillness, the three of them stand hushed and, above their heads, moths flicker around the lightbulb on soft wings.

In the pause, the dog slinks sheepishly back through the doorway in a mess of dirty paws. When she raises her low hanging head and whines, shamefaced, the problem becomes apparent. She's tried to eat a wasp. Her snout has mushroomed to double its normal size and she looks ridiculous, like a cartoon dog gone wrong. After everything in the last half an hour, it's so unexpected that Annie starts to laugh and then can't seem to stop. Jude and Dan follow, Jude resting a hand on his father's shoulder. When they finally stop for breath, Annie's cheeks are wet. She watches Dan's face split into a grin bigger than she's seen in months, shaking his head at Lena. She sees the strength of his hands as he gets up and cradles the dog's head gently.

'You silly dog.'

Those hands could hold a baby, throw a toddler giggling with delight up in the air, teach a child how to fish in the bay under the hot summer sun. And Annie thinks that maybe this could be something good.

Umbilical

Kali Napier

8.5 weeks

Chill water trickles through the cannula between the bones of my right hand. The plastic bladder pulses; an external heart.

I shudder, violently. The ER's air-con is set to freezing.

'Can I have a blanket?' I ask the nurse taking my vitals.

She swaddles me in warm, loose-weave cotton. 'Do you want an emesis bag?'

'No. Thank you.' I'm still cramping but haven't vomited for hours.

Paul brushes his hand through my fringe. A check for fever, petting me; no, he turns away to tap on his mobile phone.

'Babe, sorry?' he says. Yes, I'm still here. Teeth gritted—the cold, I swear. 'Just going outside for reception. I'll be back before the sonographer. You'll be fine.' Trailing that promise through the automatic doors.

Twenty minutes later our eyes are fixed on the screen. On the bubble.

A heartbeat, Paul. It's our baby's heartbeat. I've known it. Felt it. Though the book says I shouldn't be able to yet.

'The good news is that it's not ectopic, so you won't need to have another scan until twelve weeks,' the sonographer says. She withdraws the ultrasound wand, disgorging blue gel between my thighs. Paul grins, so she looks to me. 'And hopefully not back in Emergency. Make an appointment with radiology.'

The twelve-week mark: the first hurdle to expect when I'm expecting—according to the book I've hidden copies of both in the desk drawer at the office and in the bedside table. Out of sight. I'm not usually superstitious. But I don't want to tell. Not yet.

For now, I have a grainy image of a spit bubble inside a balloon-shaped womb. I tie it to my heart with gossamer ribbon.

12 weeks

The gel tightens the skin on my belly, prickling. I inhale slowly.

'Is that the head? It's huge. Is that normal?' Paul's first response at the forming shape of our baby.

'Perfectly normal,' says the sonographer. I feel more at ease seeing her out of blue emergency scrubs and in the lime-walled radiology suite.

I loop my wrist in the gossamer ribbon. First official scan. I can start believing she's real. I breathe out.

The pixellated womb contracts.

'Do you want to hear?' The sonographer offers us the heartbeat.

'Yes,' we say at once.

The pulse drums, breathy, sonic. 'Fast,' I say.

'That's normal. So, do you want to know?' The sonographer wields the ultrasound wand with the power to grant wishes. But I need her to run it over my slippery belly again—the foetus is no longer waving; she's frozen static on the screen.

'No,' says Paul. 'We want it to be a surprise.' *He* does. I already know she's a she, in the same way that Donna at work *knows* things.

Paul drops me at the office before lunch hour's over. Before the manager blows a gasket about productivity loss, and I'm subjected to his ranted refrain asking if I've been lobotomised. But no one has jobs they're invested in anymore. The state of the economy, mostly. Profits over people—why should we care? The entire drive, Paul talks about getting a plumber in to fix the leak near our water meter. All I can think about is our—*my*—baby, how ethereal she seems, like a deep-sea fish that's never seen the light, and caught in a globe of the thinnest blown glass.

I have to wait until the evening to tie the ultrasound image to my heart with another ribbon. There's space.

15 weeks

This was going to be the day I told work. Of course, Donna's already guessed. Rubbed my belly in the Ladies' a few days after the ultrasound.

'That's a bit rude,' I said, instinctively laying over a protective hand.

'Up the duff—I can always tell.' She lifted her chin.

I glanced at the ceiling, first instinct to tug the balloons in close. I didn't want Donna to know that I knew that *she knew*. Our friendship could break, so I hid my secrets. No one else can see the balloons. Or that I am swelling.

In our team meeting this morning, the question is in Donna's eyes; but now is not the moment to break the news. Matthew Rigley struts the floor, aggressively clicking through the slides of the PowerPoint presentation. There's been a stuff up along the line—someone's fault—and we all share the blame. What they might, elsewhere, call 'team-building'. But we don't fall into each other's arms for trust exercises—employees are always leaving. The ones who crave satisfaction from their work. As I see it, databases are databases; the figures could be toilet rolls or people's lives.

But the person really to blame for this protracted lambasting from Matthew Rigley is Mrs Rigley. The very *ex*-Mrs Rigley.

In the staff kitchen the conversations have been going like this:

'She took the keys to his Audi? No bloody wonder.'

'Apparently there's a new man.'

'Already? Jesus.'

'He's cut toilet breaks to five minutes!' (This was me. I didn't tell them why I needed to go so frequently, or how I needed to brush my teeth after retching.)

'It's nearly a year. She's entitled.'

'But he's still taking it out on us,' I say. Needs change.

'He just can't let go,' says Donna.

'Of her, or his anger?'

'Both!'

Meg from HR muses on this (though she shouldn't be standing about – hers is the busiest job of all). 'No wonder he's booked in for an op.'

'His spleen?' I ask.

'Uh-huh.'

After the team meeting, I steal an extra five minutes in the bathroom and tie double-knots in the ribbons at my heart. The balloons bob behind me back to the desk. Bounce. Bounce. Bounce. On the gyprock ceiling tiles. Bubbles pop in my belly and I still haven't told.

20 weeks

No more hiding. Since Matthew's splenectomy the office vibe is much improved; he even brought in jam doughnuts for today's meeting. Meg from HR whispered a secret—he's asked her out on a date. Donna knew already. The way she does. We all know what will happen when he eventually dumps Meg. She's a plain-looking middle-aged woman who wields her scalpel like a surgeon, relishing exit interviews.

We say nothing. I don't want Matthew bursting his stitches, bleeding through the gauze wadding under his striped shirt.

It goes without saying that Donna would know I'm not coming back after leave—she has seen the ribbons become tensile, what this means. She hasn't mentioned anything, so it's still a secret to Matthew and Meg—otherwise maternity pay will be severed, and I'll be forced to reimburse the company for training and development.

Though, as I cross off today's date on the calendar, I think: no more hiding from what's growing. *Don't buy anything for the baby until you're twenty weeks' pregnant.* Is that the book's advice? Or one of the many superstitions of the pregnancy almanac? At any rate, I'm there.

I have stuck to what to expect. Except … well, I just couldn't help myself. There was the cutest little pair of baby shoes covered in purple sequins. I bought and hid them.

But, twenty weeks … I place them on the bed, imagine her sparkling, tiny, kicking feet. Pull out the afternoon's shopping. Soon, the doona is covered in muslins, growsuits, bibs, and rattly things to fix to her ankles and wrists. Two different baby carriers. I am going to be one of those mums, bind her to me as I go about the day. The woman in the baby boutique advised that some infants prefer a sling to being carried heart to heart. To appease her, I got the sling too.

'Christ, is there anything left in the shop?' Paul's snuck up behind me. I flinch. He is unbothered by—and unaware of—the density of balloons, has no chance of becoming entangled in the web of ribbons. I'm lucky he didn't appear five minutes ago when I'd curled a floral growsuit around my swollen belly, arranging its floppy arms over hers, crossing the legs into the pretzel we'd seen in this week's scan. Not that she stays still.

Her constant rolling tugs at the anchors in my heart, changing its rhythm.

'I couldn't help myself,' I say, nudging the other bags under the valance, the pink and frilly and floral stuff. The bed is laid out in neutrals.

Paul massages my shoulders. 'That's why you stood me up for lunch, huh? I thought we agreed we'd spend more time together. While it's just us.'

His pressure's too hard, and he's treating my collarbone like tense muscle.

'I forgot.' Hunching. 'Sorry.'

Paul waves his hand over the items on the quilt. 'Wait until closer to the time, babe, or you'll get too attached.'

He means his sister's miscarriage. But that'd been early on. *Quite normal.* The lightness of her words unbelievable.

Paul is right. I pack away her trousseau, gently, and make sure to attach another balloon. Stitch the ribbon's knot in place. His real concern isn't because of his sister's miscarriage, it's because *his* ribbon has loosened. I make circles in the air with my left hand, grasp for it; there it is, cutting the circulation of my ring finger.

22.5 weeks

The ob-gyn slides the tissue box to the edge of her desk. I should not be expecting this.

'Just so you can be informed and make a decision,' she says.

The ribbons are too secure. The tides of our blood depend on them.

Paul holds my clammy left hand. To stop me from slipping.

'Tell us plainly,' he says, in control.

The name of the condition had flown my ears the moment she'd uttered it. Between Dr Wisenberg's outstretched hands I see a cat's cradle of coloured threads. As she lists off the statistics—the chances of survival—and, if then, possible life expectancy—the loops unfurl from her fingers. Then, the procedure itself.

'It's more than dilation and curettage. It's a major operation and you will need recovery time.'

All I can hear is the screeching of balloons as they bat against each other. Our hearts beat furiously.

I nod. Paul, mouth tight, grimly clenches my fingers in his fist. I have made the right decision.

23 weeks

The sky is blue. Gauzy clouds. Sun slants through the window onto the linoleum of the ward.

'You're awake.' Paul. His giant head hovers over me. Bounce. Bounce. I blink and his head reattaches to his neck, and the rest of his body, that I assume is standing beside me.

I open my mouth. Breath comes out, warm. There's an incessant beeping from the machines.

Ba-boom, ba-boom, ba-boom.

'Did it ... ?' The rest dies.

'Yep, it went well. Everyone's sent flowers and cards.'

Bright blooms fill vases at the foot of the bed. A silver foil heart-shaped balloon is tied to the chair leg. Paul notices me flinch and, as he unties the curling ribbon, it turns in the gust. I wait for *It's a girl.*

There are no words, only purple printed sequins.

I think of baby shoes, never worn.

'Donna sent it,' Paul says. 'She'll be happy to have you back at work.'

I expect a catch in the heart. Nothing. I fumble to feel the wound, but I'm connected by plastic tubing to the IV stand where a plastic bladder pumps blood. The movement jerks Paul towards me. I sneak my right hand across the blanket and find the wadding packed into the empty cavity.

I breathe in, out. Outside, beyond the glass, the bunch of balloons rises up, up, up, trailing bloody ribbons tied to the swinging lump of my still beating heart.

War Stories

Thomas Hudson

The two of them were drinking on the balcony, the last of his things moved into her apartment but not unpacked. Apart from the surfboards they'd crammed into the carport, he didn't own much and neither did she. They'd figure out where everything went, eventually, and the sun dropping behind the distant petrol station glow gave her the feeling of a day over and a job done.

'I thought this'd be a bigger deal,' he said.

'Speak for yourself. I'm gonna take a Nurofen, my back's wrecked.' She went inside, took two pills and came back with another glass of Rosé and a Cooper's Red for him. She sat down in the green plastic chair and watched him open the beer and try to start again.

'I meant, I expected it to feel like more of an occasion or something—me moving in and selling the van.'

'Were you expecting a commitment ceremony?'

He laughed. 'No, I'm trying to say, it's good this doesn't feel like a big thing. I just haven't lived with anyone for over thirty years. Haven't even lived in a house for more than ten. It always felt like a big, life-altering thing to move in with someone. This is good.'

'That's one thing I like about getting old. Not everything's a big deal if you don't want it to be.'

They were quiet for a bit. The sound of cicadas and distant traffic.

'Want to hear about the last time I tried to move house with a woman? Which is, coincidentally, the last moment I was ever in a serious relationship.'

'I don't know, do I? Talking about break-ups and divorces is like telling people about your dreams. It only feels important to the one talking.'

He laughed and it made her think of a few weeks ago, on her fifty-sixth birthday, when he said that in his whole life he'd never even had a friend as sharp as her. An odd semi-compliment she kept finding herself trying to live up to.

He went on. 'It's probably also the worst thing I've ever done as a human being.'

It felt like he'd keep talking whether she wanted him to or not and she was hit with a feeling she couldn't label. It wasn't worry—that was the whole point of this thing. This tentative friendship-*cum*-tentative relationship. An easy bonus she never counted on and, so, didn't need to count on. It was more like finally getting the full picture of how someone that smart and funny ends up being a guy who lives in his car, who smokes joints rolled with parking fine notices for a laugh, and who empties a bottle of piss into the ocean baths toilet every morning. Like knowing whatever he was about to say was for sabotaging things before the boxes were even unpacked. The next in a long line of decisions working against his interests.

'Whatever I'm thinking is probably worse than what happened, so, you might as well tell me. And I know you've been dying to ask why I've been here alone so long and what kind of skeletons I've got. So, if you feel like you need to go first, off you go mate.' She sounded colder than she meant to.

'That's not what I'm doing. But I can't lie and say I wouldn't love a clearer picture of your whole life. Even the bad bits. We've missed so much by only meeting now.'

Even the bad bits. She'd never met a man who didn't want the details of who came before. Even now, after almost 20 years alone, the only things close to male relationships were the other referees at the basketball stadium and the players who could turn from jokey acquaintance to abuser in a split second.

'And yes, I can't understand how you haven't been snapped up again. All those decades of being you,' he continued, putting his beer down and moving his chair closer.

'No, fine. I'll go first,' she said.

'No, I'm honestly not asking anything, I just had some old memories saying g'day that's all and, you're right, relationship stories—.'

She calmly cut him off. 'After all the years I spent going over things, especially after the stress haze of single parenting started to recede, do you know what I put the failure of my one and only marriage down to?'

He didn't say anything.

'Eczema.'

'Eczema? Like the rash?'

'You mean, like the nightmare.' She enjoyed his confusion for a moment.

'I had horrible eczema when I was a kid. On my face, my wrists, my legs, just everywhere. Some of my most vivid childhood memories are of lying in bed trying not to wake my Mum while I cried; fighting the urge to scratch my skin off and make things worse.'

'That sounds awful.'

'It was. But then one winter it just went away. And I never had anything like that for almost 15 years. But when we had Sarah, I think she was about 11 months old, in the space of a few days, she was just covered in it. Eczema's genetic but I still think that shitty, damp house was the trigger. Poor little thing went through hell and she was awake screaming almost hourly at night and it went on like that for nearly eight months. And she still had a mild case for almost a year after that.'

'God.'

'Me and him weren't like people any more. Eight months doesn't seem that long but we could barely function or speak to each other. And for the first two years of her life, really, he just didn't get that connection with her, you know, as a little bundle of joy. And I got it again, too. On my face and legs. I reckon from the stress and being so run down. Mine only lasted two months or so, and it was manageable, but, on top of all the worry and the sleep deprivation, I felt terrible and I could only imagine what he thought of me. Ugly, and a completely different person to who he married, I guess. And he blamed me.'

'Because it was genetic?'

'Yeah … and to have something to blame. You know what's kind of fucked about it? I used to think that if she'd had something like Leukemia, he might've pulled in close to me. Treated it like something we could put our lives together to overcome. But it was just a fuckin' common rash to him, or at least to anyone he tried to talk to about it. His world was brought down by something everyone thought of as this minor thing. Obviously, I blamed him for a long time. But it became unhealthy for me to blame him and I could never know how things might've gone without the Eczema, so, like I said, I've boiled it down to that now.'

She realised she'd been compulsively taking tiny sips of her wine as she spoke and it was gone now.

'I'm sorry you went through all that. And I'm sorry I brought it up.'

'It's fine. Anyway, technically you didn't bring it up. And I've obviously thought about it pretty hard, so maybe I wanted to spew it out like that to someone who might care. And besides, you know what else?'

'What?'

'Your turn.'

'Ah, shit, I don't want to now. Thought I was off the hook.'

'No way, fair's fair. Tell me your boring tale of cheating or cold feet or whatever.'

'Fine, but it's not that. It's much worse really.'

'Well, let's hear it.'

'God, listen to us. Two oldies trading war stories.'

'Stop stalling. I'll start you off.' She put on a dumb man's voice, 'The last time I moved house with a woman was back in—what year was it?'

'Wow, great impression. It was 'eighty-eight, or 'eighty-nine,' I can't remember. I think I was twenty-six …'

'Good, take it away.'

'I'd just turned twenty-five actually.'

'Details, get on with it.'

'Okay, I was twenty-five, we'd been living together three years, she probably thought we should've been married already. Our landlord sold up, so we had to pack up and move out fast. And, thinking back on it, I might've had sort of a nervous breakdown. Or at least my selfish version of one. I just couldn't bring myself to pack all of our crap, all our life together, put it in another house, and do it all again. She was a hoarder and we were arguing over, you know, what to keep, what to chuck. And just seeing all of her trivial things in little piles and boxes, all labelled and that. I don't know, maybe moving that much stuff just makes you a bit insane. I know I wasn't drinking enough water because we'd packed all the cups up.'

'So, you just left?'

'I got rid of most of my things, paid rent for four months so she didn't have to rush sorting out something else. But I still couldn't physically bring myself to finish the move. Her Dad came up from Sydney to help. He came looking for me and I hid. Spent the next few months in the van surfing and sulking down south, 'round Merimbula. Good bloke, hey?'

She wasn't buying the self-deprecation. 'So, you were bringing this up to sabotage this little moving-in scenario, were you?'

'No, I guess I just want to start by being honest. Talking about things.'

'Or maybe you want a medal for doing the bare minimum here today?'

He laughed quietly to himself. 'That's probably it, actually. Something like that.'

She followed his gaze off the balcony and over the rooftops, the sun gone now. Bugs buzzing around the streetlights.

'I guess I do want to say that I'm a different person now. And I like to think I got different before we met. But maybe that's just because I never went near a serious relationship again till now,' he said.

'Is this serious, is it?'

'I don't know.' He shifted in his chair, struggling to choose his next words. 'But just … I don't know, being here with you now … I just can't think of myself not finding you kind of wonderful and beautiful even if you were covered head to toe in a rash. And maybe I like the idea of sticking by you if things ever get rough again.'

She let him squirm in the silence, enjoying him unsure of himself for once. Then she made that motion like putting two fingers down your throat to vomit. 'Whatever, Romeo, you just like that I don't have much stuff.'

He cracked up laughing and she couldn't deny how wonderful things felt in that moment.

'You really do have fuck all here,' he said, laughing again.

She laughed too. The tension finding its way out. She knew she was letting something slide. Letting him off somehow. He'd made the whole thing sound so simple, so much in the past. Thirty years earlier he wouldn't have lasted that scene either and she felt guilt for that abandoned girl moving house on her own—a late betrayal of a woman she didn't know, so could only picture as her younger self. But it wasn't thirty years ago. Those circumstances were long gone. The wine had made her tired and she thought about the coffee he'd make her in the morning, doing the quiz in the paper together, and the swim they'd have in the ocean—her body weightless and painless, swimming up and wrapping itself around him.

She grabbed his hand firmly and moved it up to her neck, guiding him to where the knots were.

Curriculum Vitae

Christine Kearney

Sophia Carson is applying for a job, application due midnight. She sits at her kitchen table, slippered feet on grey linoleum, laptop open in front of her, working on her CV. She's happy to be busy, happy that this application is due tonight. The nights when there is nothing to do aren't good. Rather, she's not good on these nights. At these times she feels as if she's not so much living as waiting. Waiting for the night to pass. Waiting for morning. Waiting for the first plaintive call of the first currawong. These nights when she cannot sleep, for thinking about where she'll find a job. A recent thing—sleeplessness, joblessness.

Tonight Sophia is applying for a job in communications. She's not currently working in this field. She's not currently working in any field, has not worked since her last contract expired and she was not renewed. They let me go, she thinks as she stares at the heading in her CV which reads *Employment— Current*. It describes this last job, a six-month APS 5 in the department of industry. Nine weeks ago, she was able to list this job under *Employment— Current*. But she has not been able to do so for the past eight weeks and cannot do so tonight. A feeling of helplessness rises in her and she does her best to stave it off. If she doesn't, she knows that a whiff of desperation will somehow leach into her CV, and when it's read by a recruiter they'll detect a note of panic. A desperate applicant is never successful. She will not then be called for a chat about the role. She will not be asked about her availability. She will not be interviewed.

One letter at a time, she deletes the word *Current* so that the top section now reads *Employment*. She then goes over the four lines in which she describes her last job and the tasks for which she was responsible. She embellishes this description to make a reasonable skill set, a decent work ethic and ordinary common sense seem extraordinary, courageous, exceptional. Now to the cover letter.

At 29, Sophia has discovered that working is a breeze. Turning up presentable is nine tenths of the gig. A warm body on the chair is mostly what's required. But getting an interview is an extreme form of competitive fishing in which hundreds of people cast in the one small pool for the same little fish.

Dealing with recruiters is even worse. 'Supposing you had to paint an airplane for me,' a recruiter once said to her.

'Sorry what?'

'An airplane. It's part of your job description. I have an airplane and I want you to paint it for me. What colour would you choose?'

Fuck me, thought Sophia.

'What's the shortest contract you'd accept?' another had asked. 'Would you take three months?'

Sophia had blinked. I'd take three weeks, she thought, three days, three hours at a pinch.

'Three months? Well, it's not ideal. But I try to be as flexible as I can.'

At that, the recruiter had smiled. The right answer thought Sophia and here's hoping she remembers me—Sophia the Flexible, ready to hop in and get the job done even on a shitty three-month contract.

Sophia is racking up debts from eating, from living, from paying her rent. For the past eight weeks, her paymaster has been a pink credit card. Yesterday, with that card she bought a huge stainless steel pasta pot. It came with a lifetime guarantee and promised dinner parties in which Sophia would dish out spaghetti vongole to friends seated at a long, rustic dining table. She glances up at the pot now and winces to think that it cost almost half her weekly rent. Where do you even buy vongole? she wondered. As if! Sophia lives alone, cooks only for herself and is squeamish about raw seafood.

But I am not unemployed, she reminds herself. She's learnt never to utter that word in the small rooms a block back from Northbourne Ave where she is grilled by recruiters. Unemployment is contagion. Everyone fears it and no one in the world of recruitment is interested in ministering to the unemployed. I am a contractor, she repeats. Contractors are flexible young people who can pick up their skills and take them anywhere. Bright young people who've seen the lie of the land and have set out, keep-cup in hand, to negotiate role after role.

Sophia is not a contractor by choice. She'd prefer a permanent job. Who wouldn't? Who wouldn't want to win Powerball? But permanent jobs are like truffles, rare and precious and worth their weight in gold. Once you become a permie, there's no way, short of being run over by a Woden Express or taking a redundancy package that you'll relinquish this state. But she's learnt never to let this slip either—to be hankering after permanency might be seen as too needy. It might cause a recruiter to doubt that you would put your heart and soul into a temporary job.

'Are you interested in permanent work? Or do you like contracting?' a recruiter once asked.

'Absolutely,' Sophia laughed.

'Absolutely which?'

'Absolutely both. If the right permanent role came along, I'd be interested. But in the meantime, I'm happy working in different teams. And I really like project-based work. That's another benefit of being a contractor.'

Recruiters were none too interested in probing motivation. You could be a serial murderer gushing crap about human rights, she thought. A fraudster. Bone lazy. But if you'd mastered the art of bright, up-tempo responses and your referees checked out, they were happy to offer you up.

'I'd like to put you forward for a role,' one recruiter had said breathlessly.

When Sophia had answered the phone, she was standing in the Asian grocer with a bottle of black bean marinade in hand and kicking herself for picking the jar up in the first place. Buy essentials only, she reminded herself.

'Awesome!' she'd responded.

Never mind that the job was in Tuggeranong, in the Mordor-like wastes of the department of human suffering. Never mind that she was terrified of the Tuggeranong Parkway, of its narrowness, of the way people hurtled along it, permies in their solid family cars cars burning up fuel for which they never had to consider, essential or not?

She got an interview, and forward she drove, down the parkway to meet the EL2 who was heading up the team. Sophia was not successful, however. The EL2, a lady with a nasal voice and plum-coloured fingernails later told the recruiter she wanted someone with more intranet experience.

'But I have intranet experience,' Sophia had protested. 'Last year, I did a whole intranet proj—'

'Recent intranet experience,' the recruiter said.

Didn't want to work in Tuggeranong anyway, she reminds herself, as she fine tunes *Education* and adds a line called *Major Achievements*. She deletes the old telemarketing job for odour-free sports socks. She takes an eggbeater to the opening blurb about herself, peppering it with the words 'strategic', 'superior' and 'advanced stakeholder management'.

She would not be in this situation of course, if she'd been extended in her last job.

'Any chance of an extension?' Sophia had asked her director a month before her contract expired. She'd meant to add, 'I would love to stay on'. She'd been planning on saying this for months, but every time she and her boss stood together at the Zip hot water outlet, her courage failed her. She couldn't muster the requisite enthusiasm, couldn't chat with him the way the IT temp did of a Monday morning, dissecting the Raiders' fortunes, discussing this or that player's hamstring tear or groin injury.

'There's no budget for that position,' he'd said.

No budget for your position. For you, she thought.

'All good,' she said brightly. 'If that does change at any time—?' She laughed, waiting for him to chime in. He wants me gone, away from his desk, out of his face, she realised. She felt this almost physically, as if she were suddenly suspect, an outlier, liable to infect others with her flighty state of contract-hopping. 'If that does ever change, just let me know.'

'You're a good worker,' he offered. But this was said in the flattest of tones as if track record would have no bearing on her actual chances of being extended. He may as well have said, 'The rain in Spain.'

She returned to her desk, a placid smile on her face in case anyone else in the bay had heard their humiliating exchange. At her workstation, she began an email.

Hourosljajkalkjklj fuck fuck fuck she typed

Hiw'ouw'euriouweoi;ur;oweirfwl;kfjfck,d.lzn FAARQ

Around her, she heard the fidget click of fingers on keyboards, the sound of industry, of information being sent to and fro. Let me stay, she pleaded silently. Let me work and be paid. We're all valued members of the team, she realised, until we're not so valued. On Tuesday morning with a brief to get up to the first assistant secretary, we're valued. By Friday 5pm, we're past tense.

Don't worry about all that now. Just focus, she tells herself. You need this job. This one. It's a twelve-month contract. That's twenty six pays including the Christmas shutdown. Application due midnight.

At 11.48 she hits send and shuts down.

She goes to bed and dreams of colour, of bright squares and shapes. In the morning, she eats toast and honey at the kitchen table. She flips through the Saturday paper, pausing at the death notices. Some of the notices are brief, with just a name and a span of years. Others are letters, notes, the dearest of cards written to the loved one. As if that were still possible, the sending of a letter to that person.

To our darling Jennifer, as your 30th birthday approaches, we still cannot believe you are no longer with us. We think of you every single day with an ache that never goes away. Love always and forever, Mum, Dad, Zoe and Ben.

She thinks of her Mum, Dad and sister in Sydney. They never visited. Her mother, she suspected, had an almost visceral dislike of the capital, of its earnestness, of its refusal to man a proper CBD like Sydney or Melbourne or even Newcastle. But if something happened to me here in Canberra—she doesn't use the word 'die' but that's where she's going—they'd do one of those letters too. Every year, Mum'd send one to the paper. They'd miss me here, in Canberra. They wouldn't be able to picture me here anymore and that'd floor them. A cherished piece of this strange city somehow gone forever.

Well what of it? You're here in Canberra. Still alive. Still kicking and you need a job. You need this job. She looks up at the pasta pot hanging above her stove, a stove which is not really hers but rented along with the lino floor under her slippered feet. No matter. She remembers the colours in her dream and waits for a bite on the end of the line.

Inertia

Sue Brennan

A kitchen that's never been cooked in. Glasses shining, no smear of a lip. A sleek grey granite butcher's block. Meghan hates that name—it conjures up images of blood and gristle. The reality is a spoonful of mashed avocado on some organic sourdough and a sprinkle of cracked pepper. She leaves the fruit on the bench and eats standing on the balcony. There is an outdoor setting capable of seating six people, though this has never happened.

It's eight o'clock, and she's showered and dressed. Mark left for the gym and then work one hour ago. Since they married nine months ago, she hasn't looked for work, or joined a gym, or shopped for food, or cooked. She hasn't cleaned the toilet or even wiped a bench. The avocado on the butchers block? Vanessa, the Filipino maid, will silently put the two halves together, wrap it in plastic and place it in the fridge.

When Mark had woken this morning, she'd rolled away, cursing herself for having turned towards him during the night. She listened to him piss straight into the bowl. He'd picked up his gym bag, stretched across the bed and kissed her on the shoulder.

'See you tonight.'

'Mm.'

She knows about Echo, and now there is another one.

Echo.

Why do the Chinese give themselves such names? *Justice, Sherlock, Peach, Zero*, she's heard all of these since she arrived in Hong Kong three years ago to teach English. Her Chinese co-workers, her generation, all had names such as *Jessica, Ignatious*, and *Daphne*. It made her wonder if they'd all been reading Jane Austen novels. In the beginning, when she had a student with a name like

Cousin or *Bunny* or *Car*, she cautioned them.

'If you introduce yourself to people in Australia with that name, they're going to laugh in your face.'

After a while, though, she just stopped and thought, *good luck with that, Giraffe.*

Echo.

She found out about it at a restaurant. They were dining with one of Mark's colleagues, Peter, Australian like her and his wife, Alex. She was Québécois and much of the conversation that evening centred around this fact.

As the dinner plates were being removed and dessert being discussed—no, argued about by Mark and Alex—Mark's phone, face-up on the table between them, vibrated. Meghan automatically glanced down.

Echo: Can you make it over tonight?

Peter was looking bored, and Meghan said, 'Seriously. It's just fucking dessert. Let's get one of each and share.'

'You Australians,' Alex said. 'You're so easy-going.'

'You say that like it's a bad thing,' she said.

Mark gestured to the waiter and ordered a selection of four desserts and coffee. She watched him from the corner of her eye as he picked up the phone, input his password, typed a short message with two thumbs and put the phone in his pocket.

Echo.

Her image is of someone ethereal—long black hair hanging over one side of her face. An almond-shaped eye.

She guessed the password to his phone by watching the pattern of his fingers whenever she could. An L formation. 1478 or 2589. One evening about two weeks later, she had her chance. They'd finished eating—Vanessa had picked up some food and wine from Marks&Spencer's—and he'd gone to take a bath. She knew she had a good thirty minutes.

There were many work-related emails and, unsurprisingly, everything was sorted into folders. Mark was an organised man, something she'd teased him relentlessly about when they first met.

'It's because you're Swiss,' she'd said.

He'd taken it good-naturedly and said, 'So *all* Australians are funny because *you're* funny? Uh-huh. I see.'

Back then he'd found her very amusing, a little shocking at times, and she'd played up to it.

She pressed on the WeChat icon and scrolled through the contact list. There was only one Echo. Her profile picture was a Persian cat. She swiped her finger up and down the screen, trying to get to the starting point of the conversation, but it went on and on. Most of it was variations on a theme—arrangements for meeting up. There were lots of emojis—hearts and smiley faces—which surprised her. He rarely used them with her, even when they were dating.

She paused, walking lightly from the living room to the door of the bathroom. Mark was watching something in German on his laptop. She heard a faint slurping of the water as he wiped his nose, raised a knee. She put her head around the door, holding the phone behind her body.

'Having a long one, hey?'

'Are you waiting for it?'

'No, no.'

'You want to join me?' he said.

'After you've been sitting in it with all your filth?'

'You used to love it.'

'Another time,' she said.

Vanessa was tidying up the kitchen and preparing to take the garbage out.

Meghan sat down and resumed scrolling, The conversation was monotonous—we're meeting here, there, not meeting, missed meeting. Three months of it until she saw the photo. Ah, young, then. About twenty-five or thirty years old. Pretty, but not beautiful. A short bob cut. Almond-shaped eyes, yes. Heavily lined. Nothing ethereal about the shaved pubes and pierced nipple, though.

She contacted one of her old teaching friends, Jack, the next day. She felt guilty because since she married, she pretty much abandoned the lot of them. Jack was pleased to hear from her, and they arranged to meet that evening after he finished work.

Jack was a gorgeous, flamboyant, gay American that she got along well with in the year that they worked together at the university. He was her sounding board through the months that she first dated and then lived with Mark. He even came to their wedding. He liked Mark. Called him a babe the first time they met.

'Fucking asshole,' he said when she told him about Echo.

She nodded wetly against his chest and then got very drunk.

When she arrived home about 1am, Mark was coming out of the shower.

He looked surprised to see her and tried to kiss her on the cheek. She pushed him aside and began to take her clothes off.

'Careful, it's slippery. You seem a little … unsteady.'

'I'm fine.'

'Alright,' he said and dried himself off in the doorway. 'How was Jack? Good night?'

She stood face up under the stream of hot water. If there was one thing she loved about this apartment, it was this shower. Two years of living in a shoebox with low water pressure made every shower here a pleasure she never wanted to give up. She reached for the shampoo—*L'occitane* now that it was him paying, replacing years of cheap Pantene. When she got out of the shower, she smothered herself in *Jurlique* moisturiser. No more of that Nivea crap.

She walked naked and fragrant though the bedroom to find her pyjamas.

'Don't put them on,' he said.

She rummaged through the drawer, her back to him.

'You're so lovely.'

She found them and walked back through to the bathroom.

'Yeah, I'm a real doll.'

She heard him sigh and turn off the light. She dressed, put the lid down on the toilet and sat with her face in her hands.

'Where did you eat tonight?' she called.

'Picked up something near the office.'

'And then?'

'And then?' Come here. Come to bed.'

'I don't want to.'

'Why not?'

She picked at the cuticle around her thumb.

'How was Jack?' he asked.

'Thinking of starting a PhD'

'Good for him. Here or back in the States?'

This really was ridiculous.

She went into the bedroom. His face was lit by the screen of his phone. When he saw her, he switched it off and plugged it into the charger on the bedside table.

'Who are you texting at this time?' she asked.

'Just writing myself a reminder for tomorrow's meeting.'

He moved across when she got in, and put his hand on her stomach.

'So a bit drunk, hey?'

'Yep.'

'We used to drink a lot before we got married.'

'Yep.'

'You were a happy drunk then.'

'I was, yes.'

'Not now, though, eh?'

'Not tonight, no.'

'Okay.'

He went to roll away from her, but she held onto his hand, pressed it against her stomach and passed out.

The next morning, after he'd left for work, she went wandering through Wan Chai, her old neighbourhood. She'd immediately loved Hong Kong when she first arrived almost three years ago—the higgledy-piggledy, the mountains visible in the spaces between the spear-like buildings. She went to her old apartment building and looked up to the fifth floor—an eighteen square meter room, noise coming from every side, a broken air conditioner, mould, cockroaches, a hard bed. The first night Mark had spent there was also the last.

'I think we'll stay at my place from now on, eh?' he'd said in the morning.

She'd teased him for being soft but was secretly relieved to escape to his clean and spacious apartment. As soon as the one year rental contract was up, she'd moved in with him.

She headed towards the market she recalled. It wasn't a touristy one like those over in Kowloon with their "I ♥ HK" T-shirts and rip-off designer handbags. This one sold underpants and incense, plants and kitchen utensils. The stall owners sat on small plastic stools reading the newspaper and ignored her. She strolled towards a French bakery, ordered a coffee and cherry-pistachio financier, and sat looking out of the window. This is where they had first met. She could recall word-for-word their conversation. How easy it had been. How they'd flirted.

This is to where—when—she'd like to return. Before a beautiful apartment twenty floors up. Before a Filipino housemaid. Before a credit card she didn't need to worry about paying off.

Before a photograph of some woman's genitals.

Six months of checking his phone on the nights he takes a long bath. Six months of watching him out the corner of her eye every time he touches his phone. Six months of dinner out, dinner in, dinner with friends, dinner alone.

Six months of having sex with him, sometimes when she doesn't want to, sometimes when she does.

And now there's *Jasmine*, and another photo. Another vagina.

She knows she must do something.

She finishes the avocado and toast and brushes her fingertips over the balcony. The whole day, and a vibrant, cosmopolitan city, lies before her. She walks through the apartment to the main bedroom. Vanessa has already made up the king-sized bed and put the bathroom in order. Meghan sits on the edge of the bed, her side, and checks her nails. No need for another manicure just yet. Her hair is fine, the roots recently tended to, hiding the fact that she is, at forty-five, completely grey.

She thinks about calling her parents back in Sydney. There's only a two-hour difference, and she might catch them before they head out to the club for lunch. She remembers that there's an exhibition of Mexican silver on at the art gallery. She and Mark were planning to see it this weekend, but she could always go by herself. Jack emailed her a link regarding summer school at the university. Only a couple of months work, but it would give her a chance to get back into the system. She should send off her resume. They're planning to go to Switzerland at Christmas, so she really should look at flights for that, although Mark could always get his PA to take care of it. She listens to Vanessa humming and tapping the top of the washing machine, waiting for it to finish its cycle.

Der Kuss*

Marie McMillan

I was pretty hopeless at drawing at school, but compensated by reading about art and artists. I'd borrow art history books from Rathmines Library and pour over pages of art works, paintings and sculptures. My mother used to say I was a dreamer, with which I disagreed until I saw Rodin's *Le Penseur*, which I was delighted to learn had been initially named *Le Poète*.

On Sunday mornings my father would drive us to the Dublin-Wicklow mountains, where we'd be encouraged to hop over rocks and streams as he, sometimes, would recite Wordsworthian snatches and talk about wandering lonely as a cloud. Back home, in my vacant or pensive mood, my heart would fill with pleasure. I'd dream of that naked man deep in philosophical or poetic thought and imagine myself, naked, on a pedestal, until I was further distracted by Georgia O'Keeffe's floral paintings with their stamens and stalks, and vulvovaginal esoterica. I'd pirouette with delight over *Ballet Skirt* or *Electric Light*, take flight and levitate on finding *Pelvis with the Distance* and whirl with my clandestine photocopy of her *Plate IV Drawing No.8, 1968*, which I'd stuck to my bedroom wall.

I was uncertain of O'Keeffe's references ... two violin scrolls discussing concerti, two heads close together embraced by the dance? The latter personal interpretation suited me, for I imagined I was the regally attired Princess dancing with her Prince, until it became the fairy tale that it wasn't. My reverie jolted to reality, however, when I saw Rodin's marmoreal *The Kiss*— though I much preferred its French name, *Le Baiser*, with its plosive, bi-labial connotation. Oooh those embracing, circling bodies, those intertwining arms and legs, those almost-touching lips pursed with expectant, palpable ardour. So that's what it was about? To Hades with poetry and philosophy. My thoughts henceforth were not of the doomed adulterers, but dreams of beckoning, amorous pleasures. Who would he be? What would it be like? I couldn't wait to kiss and be kissed ... but with whom? By whom?

The longed-for realisation of my imagined desire came sooner than I had expected, for while visiting my friend Lucy Murray and her friend Miriam one Saturday afternoon, her older brother Joe and two of his school friends, Arthur and Johnno, arrived in their studded boots, thick with the muddied soil of their school's rugby pitch. An exchange of feigned, indifferent glances and the trio went up to Joe's room but returned soon after and suggested a game of Spin The Bottle to which, after some giggling and nodding, we acquiesced.

But where to find a bottle? Miriam pointed to an unopened Jameson Irish Whiskey on the sideboard. Thirstily, we eyed the golden contents through the neck of distinctive green glass but, fearful that they might spill, or worse still that the bottle might break, we didn't dare touch it. There was obviously no point in asking the prayerful, little Mrs Murray for one ... She would have been horrified. Might have read the riot act, sent for Mr Murray or, God forbid, the parish priest.

What to do? Spin a vase? But then Lucy ran to the porch and returned with an empty milk bottle. Eureka. We were ready to roll. She placed it in the middle of the rug, we formed a circle and Joe reminded us of the rules. The first two spins stopped in due course, but in front of a chair and sofa—not a schoolgirl's—leg, but soon after, with a few more vigorous whirls, Joe and Miriam were designated, left the room—closing the door with a definite bang—repaired to the hall and duly returned, shoulders hunched and blushing awkwardly. When it was Lucy and Johnno's turn, the interval in the hall was a noticeably extended one, after which they returned, shyly holding hands. A few more abortive spins and the bottle's neck paused in front of Arthur; more spins later, it halted in front of me.

When I got to the hall with its black and white lino squares, I wedged myself in between the hatstand and a mahogany table, with its vase of dusty paper daisies, overlooked by the thorn-crowned Jesus on his wooden cross and, to his left, a framed, faded, print of the stigmatic Padre Pio.

'Hi,' said Arthur, as he hopped from foot to foot in front of me.

'Hi yourself,' I replied, as he continued staring and breathing and hopping.

Why was he staring, I wondered? Was he myopic, had forgotten his glasses and was unsure of the location of my mouth or, maybe, he was a budding artist and was measuring my not-so geometric facial landscape, the bridged distance between my eyebrows or length of my nose, the precise width of my nostrils? Should I be more 'alluring', I wondered, with my shoulders against the pink and wine wallpaper. I inclined my head back, closed my eyes, opened my lips slightly—through which I hoped silent tom-tommed messages of desire were being expelled through puffs of my expectant breaths—and waited, cravingly, for what I'd so long desired ... a lustrous, golden, Klimtian-enveloping KUSS.

But there was more awkward silence. No encircling of Arthurian arms, though I knew he was close. I could hear his groaned breathing and twitched my nose from the whiff of Tato crisps, which he must have been crunching earlier. His school blazer emitted that acrid odour which emanated from wet, grimy, leather schoolbag straps and their damp embrace over the years ... More silence, as I sensed and smelt his nearness ... and then *OUCH* ... something sliced through my bottom lip and impacted.

'*OUCH!*' I yelled again.

'Is everything alright up there?' called out Mrs Murray from the depths of her faraway kitchen.

When young Dracula withdrew his dental guillotine, I shoved him away. As blood coursed around my mouth and down my chin, I was incapable of an answer.

'Yes,' growled Arthur, as he turned on his heel and returned to the spinning bottle scrum.

As I dabbed my lacerated lip and bloodied chin, my only consolation was that the voyeuristic duo (the crucified Son of God and the patron saint of adolescents and stress relief), the nailed and hanged one and his miraculously wounded companion, seemed to be haemorrhaging consolingly in tandem. With my gloved hand camouflaging my bleeding gash, I popped my head around the drawing room door and said I had to get home before dark.

For weeks after I know I suffered from PBLD—or Post Bitten Lip Disorder —which was later, thankfully, cured by a more experienced lover who licked, savoured, caressed, and valued my mouth with much restorative and curatively gentle passion.

Decades later, I censored my young children's television viewing to ensure they wouldn't see material considered too mature or unsuitable. I apparently failed though, for on kissing their Mummy good night later, both wormed their sweet little pink tongues into and around my amused one. Though gob-smacked might have better described my shocked reception. On reflection, however, I was pleased to note that the French kiss insertion was softly beguiling, rather than cuttingly incisive. As to that boorishly inept Arthur—what a pity he hadn't watched a few of those R-rated celluloid close-ups.

At a school reunion years after, I met Lucy again. Inter alia, I asked about her mother, brother and his friends.

'Oh Mina,' she said, 'Mum died soon after I left school. Johnno, to whom I'm now married, is a partner with Clifford Fox Solicitors and we have twin boys. My brother Joe did medicine and has been working with *Médecins Sans Frontières* in South Sudan for about a year.'

'I'm sorry for your loss, Lucy,' I said. 'Do send Joe my regards. But what about their other friend … the rugby-playing misogynist?'

She seemed to reflect, as she picked at one of her recalcitrant cuticles, before replying, 'Who do you mean? The rugby-playing misogynist?'

'Oh yes. Oh, that fellow. You mean that Arthur chap?

'Yes,' I replied.

'Whatever happened to him?'

'Yes, he's highly esteemed now. Don't you know? Works at the Mayo Clinic … head of haematology, I think,' she proffered.

* *DER KUSS*, German for *The Kiss*, is an oil-on-canvas painting with added gold leaf, silver and platinum, by the Austrian symbolist painter Gustav Klimt. It was painted at some point between 1907 and 1908, during the height of what scholars call his 'Golden Period'.